Violet in Bloom

A Flower Power Book

Lauren Myracle

Amulet Books · New York

The Library of Congress has cataloged the hardcover edition of this book as follows:

Myracle, Lauren, 1969–
Violet in bloom : a flower power book / by Lauren Myracle.
p. cm.
Summary: Fifth-graders Katie-Rose, Violet, Milla, and Yasaman seem to have little in common but their flower-related names, but they nurture their new friendship through a social-networking site and a campaign to have healthier snacks served at school.
ISBN 978-0-8109-8983-2 (alk. paper)
[1. Best friends—Fiction. 2. Friendship—Fiction. 3. Schools—Fiction. 4. Snack foods—Fiction. 5. Natural foods—Fiction. 6. California—Fiction.]
I. Title.
PZ7.M9955Vio 2010
[Fic]—dc22
2010024319

Paperback ISBN: 978-1-4197-0032-3

The text in this book is set in 11-point The Serif Light. The display typefaces are Annabelle, Chalet, FMRustlingBranches, RetrofitLight, Shag, and TriplexSans.

Text copyright © 2010 Lauren Myracle
Illustrations copyright © 2009–10 Christine Norrie
Book design by Maria T. Middleton

Printed and bound in U.S.A.
10 9 8 7 6 5 4 3 2 1

Amulet Books are available at special discounts when purchased in quantity for premiums and promotions as well as fundraising or educational use. Special editions can also be created to specification. For details, contact specialsales@abramsbooks.com or the address below.

ABRAMS
THE ART OF BOOKS SINCE 1949

115 West 18th Street
New York, NY 10011
www.abramsbooks.com

For **Susan Van Metre**,

who grows what she loves,

and loves what she grows.

Where flowers bloom,
so does hope.

—LADY BIRD JOHNSON

Luv ♡ Ya Bunches.com

Plant It Here! | Vi

You're Invited to a Super Fabulous Flower Power Powwow!

(And you better come, or I'll pluck your petals off one by one and crush them up and make perfume out of them. And then I'll put you in a bottle and you will live on my shelf, and I'll only let you out on special occasions, mwahahaha!)
KIDDING!

When?
Sunday,
3:00 p.m.

Where?
Katie-Rose's
Lily Pad

Guests?
Who do ya think,
ya goofs?

**So who's
in????**
Leave your
name in the
flower box to
the right!

**Flower Friends
Forever! Yaaaaay!**

Flower Box

Blog

Who's in?

me
(your hostest with the mostest, otherwise known as the grean and fabulous Katie-Rose!!!!)

Yasaman
katie-rose, ur the very first person to use the Plant It Here feature! squeeeeeeee! and of course I'll be there!

Milla
😎 Can't wait!!!!

Violet
um, why r u the GREAN and fabulous katie-rose? and u spelled it wrong, btw. it's g-r-e-e-n. like that. only, why are u green?
oh! i know! yr green with jealousy cuz we aren't there with u right this second, and that's why u threatened to PUT US IN BOTTLES AND KEEP US ON YOUR SHELF! (u do realize you're very weird, right? 👀)
but yes, you weirdie, i will be there.
c ya sunday!
luv ya bunches!!!!!

Sunday, September 18

One

Violet," her dad says.

"Dad," Violet says, meaning, *Please don't. Please?*

He shifts his gaze to the steering wheel. Violet looks out the window at Katie-Rose's house. The idling engine whispers *shhh,* while the yellow house smiles and says, *Yes. You. Come in, come in—your friends are waiting!*

"Visiting hours don't end till four. We could go see your mom, and I could bring you right back afterward."

"We're already here. My friends are counting on me." *And I'm counting on them,* she thinks. Without Katie-Rose and Camilla and Yasaman, how would she survive?

Her father sighs. "Okay, Boo. Okay."

Her fingers fumble for the door handle.

"Will you do something for me?" he asks.

Violet holds perfectly still.

"I know it's hard, the way things are right now," he says, his words like worn-out puzzle pieces. They've talked about it and talked about it, how her mom's in the hospital and what that means, but sometimes it feels like the pieces never fit together. "Just . . . you need to know that it's hard for your mom, too. Will you think about that for me, baby?"

A small animal sound escapes from inside her, because she's *always* thinking about it. Doesn't he know that? It's been a month since they moved from Atlanta to Thousand Oaks. A month since her mom was admitted to California State Regional Hospital, the best in the country for "this sort of thing," as her aunt Tanisha puts it. A month since Violet has seen her mom, or hugged her, or smelled her violet-scented *Fleur de la Fée* perfume, which she's worn since Violet was born.

When Violet found her mom—on the bad day—she smelled like *Fleur de la Fée*, but she looked like a fake person. She sat on the kitchen floor with her back against the wall and her arms hanging by her sides. Her palms faced the ceiling. Her fingers curled slackly inward.

"Thinking about it" isn't Violet's problem.

There's movement from Katie-Rose's upstairs window. Katie-Rose has pulled back her curtain and is saying something through the glass, gesturing broadly. Violet can't hear her, but knowing Katie-Rose, it's something like, "What's the holdup? Stop sitting in your car and get in here!"

Violet's heart beats faster.

Now Yasaman appears. She tries to restrain Katie-Rose, but Katie-Rose wiggles free and pounds on the glass. Yasaman makes a funny face at Violet, like *Help!*

"I think your friends want you to come in," Violet's dad says drily.

There's pressure in Violet's lungs. She hopes it's a laugh pushing its way up, but when it bursts out, it sounds more like a gasp.

"Go on," he says. He puts his hand on her knee and gives her the briefest of squeezes. "Have fun."

She scrambles out of the car. Katie-Rose has managed

to open her window, and she leans farther out than common sense would dictate.

"What's the problem?" she bellows. "Everything all right?"

"Everything's fine," Violet calls. Her ribs loosen, because she's not even lying. Everything *is* fine, or will be, just as soon as she's with her three BFFs.

asaman has always marveled at how self-possessed Violet is, so when she appears in Katie-Rose's doorway with flushed cheeks, Yasaman is surprised. Or, no, it's not the flushed cheeks. Anyone would be flushed after jogging up a flight of stairs.

It's her eyes, Yasaman decides. The color of amber, and typically just as clear, Violet's eyes seem ... clouded over. Could it have something to do with the long talk she had with her dad just now?

Violet catches Yasaman studying her, and right away

she smiles. She gives both Yasaman and Katie-Rose a hug, and when she steps back, the clouds are gone.

"Where's Milla?" she asks, scanning the room.

"That is an excellent question," Katie-Rose says, plopping down on the carpet. "Where *is* Milla?"

"Here we go again," Yasaman tells Violet under her breath.

"Why?" Violet says, grabbing a pillow and stretching out on the floor. "Is something up with Milla?"

"There better not be," Katie-Rose says.

"There *isn't*," Yasaman says. She lifts her headscarf off her shoulders and lets it spill down her back. "Katie-Rose is worried because she's not here yet, that's all."

"I'm not worried. I'm *annoyed*," Katie-Rose says. "On the Plant It Here page, I said three o'clock. It's almost three thirty, so where is she?"

"On her way?" Violet suggests.

Katie-Rose scowls. Then she tries to put her feet in Yasaman's lap, but Yasaman pushes them away, because: (a) Katie-Rose's feet are not the un-smelliest, (b) Yasaman is wearing a clean pair of jeans and prefers to keep them that way, and (c) Yasaman knows that Milla is usually

Katie-Rose's footrest. Yes, Yasaman could fill in, but Yasaman also knows that Katie-Rose doesn't really want a footrest. She wants Milla, who's supposed be here by now, but isn't. Katie-Rose loves her three best friends equally and with all her heart, but Yasaman knows Milla is the one Katie-Rose worries about most, in terms of "Eeek, what if I was wrong? What if she doesn't want to be my friend anymore?"

Katie-Rose would never worry about Yasaman in that way. Yasaman is the "counted on" friend, rock solid in every way, and realizing this gives Yasaman the quickest-ever flicker of resentment. But she banishes it. It's good to be counted on. It's excellent to be rock solid.

Yasaman firmly believes that Milla is equally rock solid, and she tells Katie-Rose so. "She's not ditching us, okay? I promise."

Katie-Rose turns a fiery red, because Yasaman has laid out Katie-Rose's true fear: that one day Milla *will* ditch them. That she'll go back to her old friends, Modessa and Quin.

But she won't. Modessa and Quin were really cruel to Katie-Rose at the beginning of the year, and that showed

Milla just how chock-full of meanness pills they are. Plus, Milla's got real friends now. Her BFFs, or rather her FFFs, which stands for "flower friends forever." Violet and Katie-Rose are flowers for obvious reasons; *yasaman* is Turkish for "jasmine"; and a camilla is a small pink flower that grows by streams.

It was so cool when they realized they were all flowers. It was like Allah, or God, planted a friendship seed in the soil of each girl's heart and said, "Bloom. It is meant to be."

"Milla will get here when she gets here, so let's change the subject," Violet suggests. "Anyone have anything they want to talk about?"

"Other than Milla being late?" Katie-Rose says darkly.

"Oh! I do!" Yasaman says. It slipped her mind in the tumble of Violet's arrival and all the "Where's Milla?" drama, but there *is* something she wants to bring up. It's an idea that came to her just this morning, and it's exciting and important.

"Hit us with it," Violet says.

"Okay. Remember last month and what happened with Milla's bobble-head turtle?"

"The Fake Incident of the Stolen Turtle, otherwise known as FIST?" Katie-Rose says. She slaps the floor. "When Modessa and Quin accused me—me!—of stealing Tally the Turtle?!"

"I think she remembers," Violet says.

"What kind of person would even *think* such a thing about *me*, sweet innocent me?" Katie-Rose sits taller. "I'll tell you what kind of person! A crazy, sick, brain-diseased person, that's who! *Two* crazy, sick, brain-diseased persons!"

"Okay, but it's over now," Yasaman says. She *might* have shown poor judgment by bringing up the Modessa/Quin yuckiness at this particular moment in time. "It was terrible and awful, but remember, we won."

"Of course we won!" Katie-Rose cries. She glances about wildly, as if someone might be hiding behind the curtains waiting to dispute this. "Flowers for justice, I tell you!!!!"

"Whoa there, Nelly," Violet says. She strokes Katie-Rose's back and speaks soothingly, the way a school nurse might address someone who's taken a nasty blow to the head. "You're safe. You're among friends. We're all friends here, 'kay?"

Katie-Rose blinks. She gazes around the room as if she's just come out of a fog, and Yasaman suppresses a groan. They're being silly, and it's kind of funny, this jokey routine of bringing Katie-Rose back to reality after one of her bursts of being overdramatic. But Yasaman would rather get back to her idea.

Violet, however, seems to be having too much fun. "That's my girl," she says to Katie-Rose. "Now. Can you tell me your name?"

"Is it ... Veronica?"

"*Ooo*. I'm sorry, but no. Want to try again?"

"Is it ... Laverne?"

At this, Yasaman does groan. "You guys! Could you please stop acting like crazy loony birds?!"

They *do* stop. They stop rather abruptly, in fact, and a pit forms in Yasaman's stomach. *Crazy loony bird? Really? That's what she had to call Violet, whose mother possibly is a crazy loony bird?*

Yet when she checks, Violet seems fine. She *might* have a wisp of cloudiness hovering over her, but with Violet, it's awfully hard to tell.

"Um, sorry," she says.

Violet shrugs. *For what?* the gesture says.

Yasaman twines the end of her *hijab* around her fingers. "I just . . . you know. Wanted to tell you my idea. Do you want to hear it or not?"

Violet nods.

Katie-Rose says, "Sure."

Yasaman swallows. "Well, after Tally the Turtle, we made a promise to do two things. Do you remember?"

Katie-Rose and Violet look at each other.

"I don't," Katie-Rose whispers. "Do you?"

Violet makes big eyes.

They giggle guiltily until Yasaman cuts them off. "One, stay FFFs forever. And two, use our flower power for *good.*"

"Oh yeah!" Katie-Rose says.

"We've done an excellent job on our first goal," Yasaman continues. "But what have we done for our second?"

"Hmm," Katie-Rose says.

"Nothing?" Violet says.

"Exactly, which is why I had my idea!" Yasaman says. "We need to come up with a plan, don't you think? For how to use our power for good?"

Violet wrinkles her brow. "Can it involve bunny rabbits?"

"What?" Yasaman says. "No."

"Steam engines?"

"No," Yasaman says. It's not like Violet to be so silly, and Yasaman is confused and slightly hurt. Violet's silliness is sure to set off Katie-Rose again, which will send the conversation whirling once more away from anything real. Does Violet not care? Even knowing that Yasaman has something she wants to say?

Katie-Rose bounces and thrusts her hand into the air. "How about forks? Or, I know—Care Bears!"

Yasaman thinks she sees guilt flit across Violet's face. But it's there, and then gone, and she can't be sure.

"Saving Care Bears from theft and torture!" Katie-Rose exclaims.

"Poor Funshine Bear," Violet says, because, like Yasaman, she knows that Katie-Rose's brother cut open her Care Bear, wedged a raw egg into the stuffing, and closed the wound with duct tape. It was for his middle school's egg drop. All the flower friends know this story.

"Bad bad Sam, and poor poor you, Katie-Rose. Were you just *so* mad?" Violet asks.

Now Yasaman is starting to guess something. Something about Violet. Violet knows Katie-Rose was mad because Katie-Rose has told the story of Funshine Bear and the egg many times. So many times that Violet herself once bopped Katie-Rose over the head with a pillow to make her hush about it.

Yasaman realizes that Violet doesn't *want* to talk about anything real. It's not that she doesn't care about Yasaman. She just needs silliness and not-real-ness today, for reasons only Violet knows.

"Omigosh, 'mad' doesn't even come close," Katie-Rose says. "I mean, seriously. Can you believe that my very own brother could commit such a heinous crime?"

"Yes," Yasaman says.

"And did I mention that Funshine Bear was my very first Care Bear ever?"

"Yes," Yasaman says.

"And held a very special place in my heart?"

"*Yes,* Katie-Rose."

"Poor Funshine Bear," Violet says. "She must have been so scared."

"Tell me about it!" Katie-Rose says indignantly. But because she's Katie-Rose, she opts instead to tell *them* about it, using her imagination to fill in the gaps of Sam's bare-bones account. She paints the key elements in vivid detail: the stony-faced firefighter atop a ladder; Funshine Bear, dangling helplessly from one fluffy yellow leg; the terrifying plunge to the asphalt below. The screams. The horror. The explosion of fur, fluff, and eggy gloop.

Yasaman gives herself over to it, though secretly she wishes that either Violet or Katie-Rose would say, *Oh! Yasaman! Your idea—we completely spaced it, didn't we?* Then they'd insist that she tell them, and they'd listen, and it wouldn't make Violet sad or bad or whatever. Because although her idea *is* real, it's made out of flower power, and she knows her FFFs are going to be just as excited as she is.

Three

Camilla

Milla can hear Yasaman, Violet, and Katie-Rose chattering as she hurries up the stairs to Katie-Rose's room. She pauses outside the door, soaking in the sight of them, and she just . . . she just feels so happy, because that's the magic of friends, *if* the friends are the right kind of friends.

Milla's FFFs are exactly the right kind of friends. They're funny and loyal and true, and seeing the three of them—Katie-Rose, laughing and beating her fist on the floor as she insists upon some point; Violet, her lips twitching; Yasaman, looking exasperated, yet amused despite herself—fills Milla with gratitude. She's the luckiest girl in the world. How did she ever get so lucky, and what can she do to tell the world thank you?

"Okay, I think we've talked enough about eggs," Yasaman says, interrupting Katie-Rose. "Can we move on? Please?"

"I wouldn't trick him into eating one, though," Katie-Rose whispers to Violet. "Well, maybe I would, because he deserves it after what he did. But I myself would never eat one."

"Thank goodness," Violet whispers back. "Raw eggs are freaky."

"Wanna know what's even more freaky?"

Milla steps into the room. "What's freaky? We're discussing freaky things?"

"Milla!" Katie-Rose cries. She hops ups, hugs her, and then spanks her fanny, grinning widely.

"Ow," Milla says. "What was *that* for?"

"Because I missed you." She flings her arms around Milla again, squeezing her tight and lifting her an inch off the ground. Katie-Rose is forever lifting people up, maybe because she's so tiny and wants to prove she's strong.

"Can't! Breathe!" Milla squeaks.

Katie-Rose drags her over to Yasaman and Violet.

"Come. Sit. Discuss," she says. "We're talking about freaky things, and now we're going to go around the circle and say what we're most afraid of in the entire multiverse."

"We are?" Yasaman says. Not for the first time, Milla thinks how beautiful Yasaman is with her dark eyes and her dark hair, almost all of which is tucked into her *hijab.* "No, we're not."

"What the heck is a multiverse?" Violet says. She nudges Milla. "And where've you been, girl?"

Milla sits down. "I got held up by my moms. Sorry."

"Held up how?" Katie-Rose says.

Milla pushes her hand through her hair. "Omigosh. Well, Mom Joyce's supposed to go to this baby shower, okay? Only Sara—she's the woman who's pregnant—isn't having a regular baby shower. She's having something called a blessing way."

"A *blessing way*?" Violet says.

"Each guest is supposed to bring a homemade bead, and at the party, all the beads are going to be strung on a necklace." She rolls her eyes. "Mom Joyce and Mom Abigail were fighting about Mom Joyce's bead. I was like, 'You guys! Seriously?'"

"Why were they fighting about the bead?" Yasaman asks. "Was it ugly?"

"Um, yes, but it was more cute-ugly than *ugly*-ugly." Milla giggles, remembering the wizened lump of clay. "It was all wrinkly like a raisin. Maybe it got too dried up? And then Mom Joyce just had to paint it brown, which I don't get. She refused to paint it pink or blue . . . but brown?"

Katie-Rose scrunches her nose. "So what you're saying—correct me if I'm wrong—is that your mom made a bead the size of a raisin, and then she painted it brown, the color of a raisin. What if the baby tries to eat it? And dies?"

"It's not for the baby, it's for the mom. All the beads are going to go on a 'labor necklace,' and at the party, the guests are going to"—Milla concentrates, wanting to get the wording right—"they're going to honor the unborn baby through singing and spoken blessings."

Everyone absorbs this.

"California is *weird*," Violet pronounces.

"No, this Sara person is weird," Katie-Rose argues.

"That's what Mom Joyce says," Milla says. "She was all, 'Did I *ask* to honor the unborn baby through singing and spoken blessings? No. No, I did not.' And then something about, 'Just wait till she has an actual newborn to take care of. *Then* she'll be using Huggies, I guarantee you.'"

"Newborns! Oh!" Katie-Rose yelps. "*Max is getting a baby gerbil!* Isn't that so exciting? He's at the pet store right now!"

Max is Katie-Rose's neighbor, and he goes to Rivendell, and he's a fifth grader, like the flower friends. He's also Milla's crush. He also has really fresh breath, which smells like the same kind of toothpaste Milla uses. *Colgate, the Great Regular Flavor.*

Normally, the merest mention of Max would make Milla blush and giggle uncontrollably. Today, however, the rest of what Katie-Rose said distracts her so much that she feels faint.

"A . . . gerbil?" she says.

"Or maybe he said a hamster. Does anyone know the difference?"

"Hamsters don't have tails," Violet says. "And hamsters are the ones that have those chubby, chubby cheeks."

Milla's stomach turns. She sees a chubby-cheeked hamster in her mind, supersize and larger than a house, and she draws her knees to her chest and hunches over them. "Yasaman, do you still want to know what my biggest fear is?"

"Um, actually, I was never the one—"

"*Rodents.* All rodents, but hamsters in particular, because of those chubby cheeks, and because they have those teeth that come out over their jaws." She juts her own teeth out and over her bottom lip without consciously intending to. She shudders.

"Rats are rodents," Katie-Rose points out. "Are you more freaked out by hamsters than *rats*?" She doesn't give Milla time to answer. "I think hamsters are cute. What scares me are chickens."

"Chickens?!" Violet says. "My gran-gran has chickens, back in Georgia. Chickens aren't scary."

"Also, Michael Jackson's ghost," Katie-Rose continues. She nods. "Yep, chickens and Michael Jackson's ghost, because that 'Thriller' video is disturbing." She prods Violet with her foot. "What about you?"

Violet blinks. "Me? Um, what do you mean, what about me?"

"Stall-ing!" Katie-Rose sings.

Milla tilts her head. Violet isn't shifting or fidgeting—in fact, she seems to be keeping her muscles deliberately relaxed—and yet it's clear she doesn't like the question.

"She's not stalling," Milla says. She bumps Violet's shoulder. "She's just *Violet*. She's not afraid of anything, right?"

Violet gives her a grateful look. It flickers across her face as quick as a moth, and then it's gone.

"Yeah, whatever," Katie-Rose says, unaware of whatever just happened between Milla and Violet, and unimpressed with Violet's nonresponse. "Yasaman, what are you scared of?"

Yasaman looks from girl to girl. In a soft voice, she confesses that she's afraid her house might catch on fire while she's taking a shower and she'd have to run out naked.

"Omigoodness," Milla says, knowing that starting now, this will be one of her fears as well.

"Now *that's* a good one," Katie-Rose acknowledges. "Wow. Would you have time to grab a towel, at least?"

Yasaman lifts her shoulders in a way that's both anxious and cute. "Maybe, but maybe not."

The conversation gets loud as everyone discusses the horrifying nature of nakedness, and it's giggly and fun and makes Milla feel lucky all over again. Lucky to have her flower friends, and lucky to be neither naked, nor in the shower, nor in a house fire. *Eeeeee.*

She notices something curious, though. With all the chatter, Violet never does say what she's afraid of. Milla is probably wrong, but she wonders, briefly, if Violet's biggest fear might be telling her FFFs what her biggest fear is.

four

Around the time her friends have to go home, Katie-Rose hears Max's mom's SUV pulling into their driveway. *Max's* driveway, not Katie-Rose's. She hops up, runs to her window, and calls, "Max! Did you get your gerbil, or hamster, or whatever? Do you want to bring him over? Milla's here!"

"Katie-*Rose!*" Milla cries, aghast.

"What? You know you like him!"

"Omigoodness, please tell me Max didn't hear that. Please please please say he didn't hear."

"I don't know," Katie-Rose says, frowning at the red

minivan pulling into her own driveway. "But your mom's here. Darn."

"Thank you, Lord," Milla says to the heavens, scrambling to her feet and dashing out.

Violet's dad shows up right behind Milla's mom, so she leaves, too. Then it's just Katie-Rose and Yasaman.

"Do you want to go see Max's hamster-slash-gerbil?" Katie-Rose asks Yasaman hopefully.

"Um, kind of—but my dad's going to be here any minute," Yasaman says. "Can I please tell you about my flower power idea?"

"One sec," Katie-Rose says. To Max, who is still in his driveway, she hollers, "I'm coming over soon. Keep your pants on, 'kay?"

Outside, a car honks.

"Oh, poot. It's your dad. Why must everyone burst my bubble? Why?!"

Yasaman sighs. "Fine, I'll tell you later," she says, standing and gathering her things.

Only then does Katie-Rose realize that *she* might be bursting *Yasaman's* bubble. Clutching Yasaman, she says, "No, tell me now. I want to hear your idea, I really do!"

"You could have fooled me," Yasaman says.

"Tell me, or I'll feel like the worst friend ever."

"You're not the worst friend ever," she says. She looks at Katie-Rose with fond exasperation. "I'll email you, okay? Or—I know! I'll write a blog about it."

"And post it to LuvYaBunches.com?"

Yasaman makes a face that says, *Where else?* Then she scoots out of the house before her father has to honk again.

So technically, everything got worked out, but Katie-Rose still feels guilty as she walks over to Max's. She should have let Yasaman tell her about her flower power plan, even though, personally, Katie-Rose thinks she and her FFFs have *already* used their flower power for the greater good, simply by existing. They are the flower power fearsome foursome! *Yeah!* All Katie-Rose ever wanted was a forever friend, and now she has three. It's mind-boggling.

But friends are supposed to let one another talk and not always hog the conversation, which is something Katie-Rose's mom is always harping on her about. *Hmm.* Maybe Katie-Rose needs to go to Attention Hogs

Anonymous. Maybe she could get pamphlets and a cool AHA T-shirt, which she would totally wear, because she's all about cool T-shirts.

She reaches Max's house, but before going any farther, she makes a private vow to do better in the attention-hogging department. *There*. Then she strides to Max's door, where she's greeted by Max before she even has time to knock. He grins and joins her on the stoop, holding a furry, nose-twitching herbil-slash-gamster. *Gerbil-slash-hamster. Ag!*

"This is Stewy," he says proudly. "Here, take him."

Katie-Rose sits down and holds Stewy in her lap. "Hi, Stewy." She pets him. "Is Stewy a hamster or a gerbil?"

"Hamster. Isn't he cute?"

"*So* cute." His fur has a reddish tint, and his nose is twitchy, like a rabbit's. His top teeth do jut out over his jaw, making him look just a little bit hamster-vampire-ish. His claws are scrabbly on Katie-Rose's thighs, even through her jeans, and it feels funny. A millisecond later, something else feels funny. Warm funny. Runny funny. Not funny at all, actually.

"He peed on me!" Katie-Rose squeals, lifting him off her.

Max laughs. "It's just hamster pee. But you can give him back if it grosses you out."

It does gross her out, but Katie-Rose is stubborn about not being a girly-girl, so she resettles him in her lap. *But you better not pee on me again,* she tells him telepathically. *Peeing on people is yucky and shows bad manners, mister.*

Stewy regards her intently. His eyes are beady and strangely shiny.

"Um…does Stewy know what I'm thinking?" she asks.

Max tilts his head. His bottlebrush hair is sticking up, as always, but for Max, he looks pretty good. He's wearing nice jeans with his "I Read Banned Books" shirt, which Milla once complimented. Katie-Rose wonders if Max ran to his room and put it on when she yelled out her window about Milla being there.

"I don't know," he says. "He might, I guess. He *is* a domesticated animal."

"Why would being a domesticated animal mean he could read my mind?"

"I didn't say 'read your mind.' That would be ESP. I never said Stewy has ESP."

"Oka-a-a-y."

"It would be cool if he did, though." Max takes Stewy's bullet-shaped head in his hands and looks at him. He tries to hold Stewy's gaze, but Stewy doesn't cooperate.

"Pfff," Max says, releasing him.

"What'd you say to him? Or rather, what'd you *try* to say to him?"

"I gave him a very simple math problem and told him to blink the answer."

"Well, Max, that just means Stewy's bad at math. It doesn't prove anything one way or another about ESP."

Glumly, Max shakes his head.

"Forget ESP and explain what you were talking about before, about being domesticated," Katie-Rose says. She thrusts Stewy at Max. "And here, I'm done."

Max nestles Stewy against his chest, and Katie-Rose knows that if Milla were here, she would melt. Afterward, Katie-Rose would tease Milla about it, and it would be one more thing gluing the two of them together. Katie-Rose would like that, because there's a secret no one knows, and it's that sometimes she worries Milla will decide not to be friends with her anymore. Like, Milla might realize Katie-Rose is too boring, or bossy, or unstylish. Or maybe Katie-Rose will have a booger in her nose and not know it, and Milla will think *ew*, and that'll be the end of it.

Ha ha, you thought you were good enough for someone as cool as Milla? Wrong! Buzzzzzz! You big dummy.

Earlier, when the FFFs were sharing their biggest fears, Katie-Rose lied. Her biggest fear isn't Michael Jackson, or Michael Jackson's ghost, or chickens. Her biggest fear is being alone, like she used to be.

Beside her, Max strokes Stewy.

"Are you going to explain about the domesticated animals?" she asks him.

"Oh, right," Max says. He dives into an explanation about how in the olden days, when evolution was happening, dogs learned to survive by (a) being cute and (b) learning how to read their masters' emotions. And not just read them, but *care*, in their doggy way. Like by wagging their tales when their masters were happy, or resting their heads on their masters' laps when their masters were sad.

"That's why people say that a dog is a man's best friend," Max says.

"What about a woman?" Katie-Rose asks. "Who's her best friend?"

"Um, another dog?"

"Then the saying should be 'A dog is a *human's* best friend,' Katie-Rose says. Except she doesn't want a dog to be her best friend, now *or* when she's a woman.

Max shrugs. "Okay."

"Is there more about the domesticated-ness, or is that all?"

"That's all. Except maybe the same thing happened with other domesticated animals as well. Like cats, and possibly hamsters."

"Okay, but Stewy isn't my pet," Katie-Rose says. "He's yours. So I bet he can only tell what *you're* thinking."

Max holds Stewy away from his body so they can face each other.

"You're probably right," he concedes.

Of course I'm right, Katie-Rose thinks. *I'm always right ... except when I'm not.*

She stands and stretches. Maybe Yasaman's posted her blog entry by now.

"So . . . Milla's not coming over?" Max says.

"Milla left a long time ago," Katie-Rose says. She tilts her head, because while Katie-Rose knows Milla has a crush on Max, she doesn't know for sure if Max has a crush on her. "Do you like Milla, Max?"

"Sure I like her."

"You know what I mean. Do you *like* her like her?"

Max pats Stewy slightly harder than perhaps Stewy wants. Stewy hunkers down.

"It's perfectly normal," Katie-Rose says. She recalls a claim made by another boy in their grade. "Chance says he has seventeen girlfriends, all in different states. If Chance has seventeen girlfriends, you're allowed to have one."

Max keeps patting. Stewy's head sinks lower and lower.

"He's not a nail," Katie-Rose says. "You don't have to pound him into the ground."

Max stops. "Sorry, Stewy."

Stewy stays hunched for a moment, then reinflates. Max and Katie-Rose laugh.

"But, Max," Katie-Rose says, remembering what it is she needs to say. She eyes Max sternly.

"Yeah?"

"About Milla. She's my friend first, and your girlfriend second. Got it?"

Color spreads up from his neck. "She's not my girlfriend. Jeez."

"I'm just saying," Katie-Rose says. She leaps down his front steps, then checks to make sure nobody's pulling out of the driveway before returning to her own house. You just can't be too careful, even in your own neighborhood, because one wrong move and *splat*. You're a goner.

❈ Five ❈

Yasaman's *baba* has lots of rules, like how Yasaman isn't allowed to talk on the phone after eight o'clock, and also how she isn't allowed to get her ears pierced until she's twelve. The ear piercing rule doesn't really bother her, though. Natalia, a girl at school, has gotten her ears pierced three different times now, and each time, the holes have gotten infected, and Natalia had to let them close up so they could heal.

Yasaman saw Natalia's earlobes in their infected stage. They were red and puffy, and Yasaman felt sorry for Natalia. Plus Natalia has to wear a ginormous headgear, and Yasaman feels sorry for her about that, too. It's some sort of newfangled "super" headgear that involves a chin brace and a forehead brace and a halo of wire that circles her whole head. Natalia told Yasaman it'll fix her lisp "ten thouthand timeth fathter" than an old-fashioned headgear, and Yasaman nodded politely and said, "That's great, Natalia."

But she thought, *If I ever have to wear a headgear, please let it be the old-fashioned kind, and please, Allah, let me only have to wear it at night.*

She'd rather have no headgear, of course, just as she'd rather have no phone restrictions. But here's the thing. While Yasaman isn't allowed on the phone after eight o'clock, her *baba* never said anything about blogging.

She sits in front of her computer and goes to LuvYaBunches.com, the website she designed exclusively for the four flower friends. It's got tons of cool features, like video uploading, blog pages, a Plant It Here page for sending out fun invites or group messages, and the Flower Box, a chat room for when all four FFFs are online at the same time.

"How did you learn how to do that?" Katie-Rose asked when Yasaman first showed her the site.

"I took a class at the Muslim youth center," Yasaman answered matter-of-factly. She's good with computers, just as she's *not* so good at group work, or anything that involves standing up in front of a bunch of people and making words come out of her mouth.

She's working on that, however. If she wants to make a difference in the world, she has to be willing to take a stand—and that's where her flower power idea comes in. The idea she wanted to tell her friends about at Katie-Rose's house, but didn't, because she was incapable of slapping her hands together and saying, "HEY! PEEPS! LISTEN UP!"

No big deal. She'll tell them about it now. She takes a moment to enjoy the delicious anticipation that comes before putting words to paper—or words to screen—and then starts typing.

Blog

 Time to Girl Up!

Hello, girlfriends! Yasaman here. Ha ha, u already knew that. But here I am with my friend the frog, whom I have decided to call Siggy. Say "hi," Siggy! (HI!)

35

So guess what? After I left Katie-Rose's, the day took a turn for the worse, and it *almost* ended disastrously. More on that soon. But first, check out the special smiley I made in honor of Max's new hamster. 🐹🐹🐹🐹🐹🐹🐹🐹

ISN'T IT SO ADORABLE? Oh. Sorry. Forgot to turn off caps lock. +lowers voice to an urgent whisper+ Isn't it so adorable????!

Katie-Rose, did you get to meet Max's real-life hamster after we left? And did we decide for sure if it IS a hamster? Either way, I hope it's a nice one, cuz there's a hamster in Nigar's preschool class, and it bites! It bit Nigar's friend Lucy, who's one of the Tuesday/Thursday preschoolers. I wish Lucy went five days a week, like Nigar, cuz I know Nigar would be happier about going if Lucy was always there.

Anyway, Lucy had a playdate with Nigar today, so she was at our house when I got home. This was when the disastrousness started. I was babysitting them while my mom and dad went to Akmarket, and they were supposed to be having a dance party in Nigar's room while I read *Parties and Potions*.

But suddenly, CRASH! Then came worried whispers. Then Nigar called out very loudly in her innocent voice, "Uh-oh! Accident!"

Now, one thing I can tell you about Nigar's innocent voice is that when she uses it, she's anything but innocent. I can also tell you that Nigar's innocent voice *and* the crashing sound came from my parents' room, not Nigar's. This did not fill me with feelings of delight, let me tell you.

"Hurry, Yasaman!" Nigar yelled, even though I was already on the way. "Lucy says she's not allowed to step in glass!" (And this is off the subject, but who *would* be allowed to step in broken glass? "Yes, honey, you may have graham crackers and apple juice, and you may step in broken glass. But under no condition may you make origami!" I mean, right?)

Anyway, Nigar and Lucy had snuck into my parents' bathroom, and Lucy had dropped a bottle of my mom's perfume onto the hard tile floor. OH. MY. GOSH. The whole house stank like you wouldn't believe.

(Katie-Rose, it made me think of your plan to turn *us* into perfume if we ever disobey you, because if we wanted to escape, that's what we'd have to do. We'd have to fling ourselves off the shelf and spill everywhere!)

I told Nigar and Lucy go to Nigar's room, and I cleaned up the glass shards, but I couldn't make the smell go away, even though I opened all the windows. Plus, my mom's perfume was g-o-n-e, gone, and there was nothing I could do about that.

Fast-forward half an hour to when my parents came home. The minute my dad walked in the door, he made a face and said, "What is that horrible odor?"

Omigosh, my stomach was so nervous. I stepped forward to tell them what happened, but Nigar beat me to it, popping out from upstairs and yelling, "I'm sorry, *Ana*! I spilled your beautiful pur-foom that smells so beautiful! Apology accepted? Apology accepted. Okay!"

She has learned a lot about "apology accepted" at preschool.

Well, my mom raised her eyebrows at me, and I explained the full story. My dad was mad, but my mom laughed and said, "Oh, Ahmet, don't be a poopy."

Yes, my mother called my father a poopy. Well, in Turkish, but still.

And are you ready for the happy ending?

My mom said, "Yasaman, your grandmother gave that perfume to me, and I have never liked it. So don't worry. I'm not angry."

So I didn't get in trouble, and my mom never has to use that bad perfume again!!!!!!

Anyway, the whole incident got me thinking. About what, you ask? Well, about Nigar and Lucy and friends and flowers and sadness and happiness and . . . just EVERYTHING, including the idea I wanted to tell you guys at Katie-Rose's house. About how we need to use our flower power for good, remember? So turn your listening ears on, cuz here is the great idea I've been wanting and wanting to tell you: We—all 4 of us—are going to launch a Snack Attack!!!

The good guys: us, of course.

The enemy: those yucky Cheezy D'lites the teachers give us for morning snack, which as u know—because I told you!—are filled to the brim with partially hydrogenated soybean and/or cottonseed oils. Milla and Violet, remember that day last month when I was accidentally-on-purpose eavesdropping on you two, because you were talking about Medusa and Tally the Turtle? And I was pretending to be on a snack-getting mission for Ms. Perez, only I spilled the entire box, and Cheezy D'lites went everywhere? Well, before the big mess happened, I spent A LOT of time pretending to read the list of ingredients, and during all that pretending, I actually *did* read the list of ingredients, which is why those partially hydrogenated oils are stuck in my brain, and I've done even more research on them since then, and they are not even real food. They are FAKE FOOD. And doctors are saying that if kids keep eating fake food all their lives, then everyone's going to get really fat and have heart problems and basically every kind of yucky problem you can imagine! That just makes me SO SAD. Doesn't it make you so sad, too? Knowing that for the first time in centuries, doctors are saying that today's kids are likely to have shorter lives than their parents?!!!

I love life! I don't want to have a shorter life than I could have just because of icky fake Cheezy D'lites, and I know you guys don't, either. And together I know we can come up with an awesometatiousful plan for making Rivendell a Cheezy D'lite Free Zone! ✿ ✿ ✿ ✿

Are you with me? Cuz WE ARE WHAT WE EAT, and I, for one, have zero desire to be a partially hydrogenated soybean and/or cottonseed oil. Oh, and they're also feeding those yucky things to preschoolers, you know! Who are young and innocent!!!

And now, over and out! Byeeeeeeee! Cya 2morrow!!!!

Six

Camilla

That Yasaman is so cute, Milla thinks after reading Yasaman's blog. Well, "cute" isn't the right word. Cute is for puppies and kittens and the laughing baby from YouTube that Katie-Rose showed her.

Katie-Rose also showed her a video of a woman who can pop her eyes totally out of her eye sockets. First the woman is her normal self, and then she concentrates, and her eyeballs pop out. There are toys like that, where you squeeze the toy and its eyes bulge out like gumballs. The woman was a human version of that.

Katie-Rose is a YouTube-aholic, because making videos is her passion.

Yasaman's passion is . . . *hmm*. How would Milla describe it? Blogging, and computers, but also defending the innocent, like when those boys in Nigar's class bullied her and called her names. Maybe her passion is to make the world a better place, plain and simple, using whatever means she can?

As for the Cheezy D'lites, Milla doesn't have a strong opinion about them. She doesn't love them, but she eats them when they're given to her. They *are* an unnatural shade of orange, however. And yet she must admit that the thought of making Rivendell a Cheezy D'lite Free Zone has honestly never crossed her mind.

But what the heck. It's *Yasaman*. If Yasaman wants to do this, then Milla will help.

In fact . . .

Mom Joyce returned from her colleague's baby shower—scratch that, her *blessing way*—with party favors. There'd been a game involving tasting unlabeled jars of baby food, and Mom Joyce won, correctly identifying all the flavors including the wild card, butternut squash. Her prize? A gift basket filled with products from Yummy Tummy, an organic grocery.

When Mom Joyce got home, she deposited the basket on the granite island in the kitchen, inviting Mom Abigail and Milla to help themselves.

"Take anything you want," she said drily. "Anything. Really."

So Milla sampled a low-sugar carrot cake muffin and felt neither here nor there about it. But there'd been tons more samples in the basket. All sorts of things, all healthy.

Good feelings tingle through Milla as she posts a comment to Yasaman's blog:

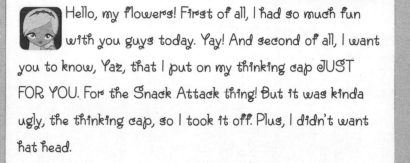

Blog

Hello, my flowers! First of all, I had so much fun with you guys today. Yay! And second of all, I want you to know, Yaz, that I put on my thinking cap JUST FOR YOU. For the Snack Attack thing! But it was kinda ugly, the thinking cap, so I took it off. Plus, I didn't want hat head.

But I came up with an idea for the Snack Attack anyway! I'm not gonna tell you what it is, cuz it's TOP

SEKRIT, and cuz I know it'll drive Katie-Rose crazy not knowing. +waves at Katie-Rose+ Hi, Katie-Rose! I have a secret, ha ha ha!

I'll tell you at lunch tomorrow, and there will be showing involved, too. Show-and-tell!

Hugs and kisses,

MarshMilla ♥

Monday, September 19

Seven

Katie-Rose

When it comes to video cameras and making movies, Katie-Rose was born ready. Her mom says she came out of the womb yelling "Action!" and clapping a baby-size director's clapboard, but *ha ha*, that isn't really true. Katie-Rose wishes it were. That would have been hilarious.

Katie-Rose is set up quite nicely, however. While she doesn't own a director's clapboard, she does have a sunshine yellow video camera. It's small enough to fit in her pocket, which means she can bring it anywhere and whip it out whenever she needs it. Like right now.

A grin spreads across Katie-Rose's face. She's ready, she's set ... *it's go time.*

FADE IN:

INTERIOR RIVENDELL ELEMENTARY—HALLWAY BY SNACK CABINET—MORNING

> KATIE-ROSE (off-screen)
> All right, Yazalicious. We have five minutes before class. Make me proud, sweetheart!

Yasaman stands, giggling, in front of a row of stacked cabinets. Her arms are wrapped around her ribs and her shoulders are up by her ears.

> YASAMAN
> Katie-*Rose*!

> KATIE-ROSE (off-screen)
> Hey, you said you wanted to talk about trans fats, so talk. You *do* want the role, don't you?

On three ... two ... one ... start!

Still giggling, Yasaman gestures behind her.

YASAMAN

Well, here we have ... the snack cabinet.

KATIE-ROSE (off-screen)

Yes, Yaz. Now get to the good part.

YASAMAN

And inside the snack cabinet, you will find ...

She opens the uppermost cabinet to reveal boxes
upon boxes of generic cheese crackers, called Cheezy
D'lites.

YASAMAN (CONT'D)

Well ... snacks.

The image jiggles. Off-screen, Katie-Rose can be heard
laughing.

YASAMAN (CONT'D)

Katie-Rose!

KATIE-ROSE (off-screen)

Sorry. Temporarily overwhelmed by your brilliance, that's all. Carry on!

Yasaman presses her lips together.

YASAMAN

But you should know that these Cheezy D'lites, while they may look yummy—

KATIE-ROSE (off-screen)

(interrupting)

And taste yummy. *Mmm*.

YASAMAN

—are actually poison disguised as cheesy goodness.

Katie-Rose rotates the camera toward herself. Her face, when it appears, is huge.

KATIE-ROSE

I came up with that, by the way. "Poison disguised as cheesy goodness."

Yasaman clears her throat. The camera swings back.

YASAMAN

And they're bad for you. That's all. Because they have trans fats in them, which lead to cancer—

KATIE-ROSE (off-screen)

And fatness! And heart attacks! And—

The image jiggles.

KATIE-ROSE (off-screen, CONT'D)
(passing the camera off to Yasaman)
Here, take this.

When Katie-Rose first comes into view, she is blurry. Then her edges pull together. She's wearing tattered jeans and a T-shirt that says "Brothers Make Good Pets."

KATIE-ROSE (CONT'D)

And they are bad, bad, baddy bad-bad, and that's all you need to know, except that we, the students of Rivendell, are the future of America!

YASAMAN (off-screen)

(under her breath)

Oh dear.

KATIE-ROSE

Do our teachers want to kill us? Is that their devious plan? Or are they simply too cheap to buy a bunch of bananas? Whatever the dark truth is, action must be taken!

She disappears, then reappears with her backpack.

Balancing it on her raised knee, she unzips the front pocket and pulls out a roll of black-and-yellow police tape.

YASAMAN (off-screen)

Um, Katie-Rose? What are you ...?

Katie-Rose rips off a piece and sticks it from one edge of the snack cabinet to the other.

KATIE-ROSE

Take that, trans fattiness!

She does a fancy karate kick and whips her arm through the air like an ax.

KATIE-ROSE (CONT'D)

Kai-yah!

YASAMAN (off-screen)

Okay, but I'm not sure how—

More karate-ness happens, accompanied by sound effects, wild eyes, and exciting arm slashes.

KATIE-ROSE

Let's see you be trans fatty now! *Mwahaha!*

At that moment, a girl in a humongous headgear comes around the corner. Neither Yasaman nor Katie-Rose spots her. She approaches just as Katie-Rose moves into a fancy lunge-and-strike sequence.

NATALIA

(coming right up behind Katie-Rose)
Hi! What'cha doing?

Katie-Rose jumps and screams. Natalia giggles.

KATIE-ROSE

Natalia!

NATALIA

Oopthie. Did I thcare you?

KATIE-ROSE

You shouldn't sneak up on people! Don't you know that's *rude*?!

YASAMAN (off-screen)

Um, hi, Natalia. And Katie-Rose, I'm sure she didn't mean to.

NATALIA

Of courth not. You jutht didn't thee me becauth you were ... doing whatever you were doing.
(more giggles)
What *were* you doing?

Red splotches rise on Katie-Rose's face.

KATIE-ROSE

It was kah-rah-*tay*, which, if you don't know, is an ancient form of self-defense that can take down even the most fearsome enemy.

NATALIA

Oh. Who'th the enemy? The thnack cabinet?

Off-screen, Yasaman tries to stifle a laugh. Katie-Rose glares: first at Yasaman, and then at Natalia.

KATIE-ROSE

Yes, thanks for mocking me. I certainly do love to be mocked. And now, good-bye.

YASAMAN (off-screen)

Katie-Rose!

KATIE-ROSE

What? I call 'em as I see 'em, all right?

YASAMAN (off-screen)

Oh my goodness. Natalia, I am *so* sorry—and so is Katie-Rose. Really.

KATIE-ROSE

No, I'm not. And, omigosh, are you still filming???

Turn off the camera, Yasaman! Now!

Natalia's eyebrows go up.

NATALIA

(to Yasaman)

Wow. Does she always talk to you like that?

Yasaman shuts off the camera, but not before capturing Katie-Rose's expression, which is a mix of defiance and unease.

FADE TO BLACK

"Here," Yasaman says, handing Katie-Rose her camera without looking at her.

Katie-Rose realizes she's messed up, though she doesn't really think it's her fault. Nonetheless, she says in a pinched prune voice, "I didn't mean to be rude. To either of you." She focuses on Natalia's shirt rather than looking directly at Natalia. "But, Natalia, you disrupted a very critical film project."

"Well, you're throwing a very critical fitical," Natalia responds.

Katie-Rose wants to slap her. Seriously. In her normal life, Katie-Rose isn't a violent person, but when she gets mad, something goes screwy in her wiring. Her thoughts go too fast. Everything is stupid. Everyone should just go away.

(Everyone who isn't one of her flower friends, that is.)

She stares Natalia dead in the eye. "'Fitical' isn't a word."

"Okay," Natalia says nonchalantly. "Why did you tape shut the cabinet?"

"Because we wanted to," Katie-Rose says.

"Well, *you* wanted to," Yasaman says, toeing the floor.

Katie-Rose's hands curl into fists.

"But why?" Natalia presses.

"Because there is trans-fatty badness going on in there."

"In the cabinet?"

"Yes. And again I say good-bye."

"Katie-*Rose*," Yasaman says helplessly, and Katie-Rose burns with shame. Does Yasaman think Katie-Rose likes being such a brat? But Natalia is being a brat, too, the way she's deliberately pushing Katie-Rose's buttons.

"We're starting a campaign," Yasaman explains to Natalia.

"Cool. For what?" When Natalia talks, the rubber bands attached to her headgear stretch. It's an extremely complicated contraption, and Katie-Rose has wondered in the past if Natalia feels the way dogs do when they have to wear those cones around their heads. She has even—IN THE PAST—entertained the idea of randomly bringing Natalia ice cream, or some other treat, just to be nice.

No more.

Today she wants to attach a hook to Natalia's headgear. A hook attached to a chain, and on the other end of the chain, an electronic pulley. Using a remote control On switch, Katie-Rose would activate the pulley, and *whoosh!* Away Natalia would go, jerked backward like a measuring tape retracting into its square metal case.

"For how we should have healthy snacks during morning break," Yasaman tells Natalia. "The Cheezy

D'lites they give us? They have trans fats, and I don't know if you know, but trans fats are super unhealthy."

"Oh, I know, I *hate* tranth fatth!" Natalia says. "Can I be part of the campaign, too?"

"No," Katie-Rose starts to say, but she manages to swallow it. Yasaman is so nice that it makes Katie-Rose feel un-nice, which is an itchy way to feel. Like having a wedgie, or when the seam of her socks scrunches up wrong.

Yasaman glances at Katie-Rose. "Um, sure, I guess. But we haven't planned it all the way out yet."

"Well, I am your girl, then, becauth I am very contherned about health. For eckthample, did you know that I've never had a Coke in my life? In my *whole entire life*?"

What?! Katie-Rose thinks. She feels her face go scrunchy, because she doesn't believe this for a second.

"Wow," Yasaman asks. "How come?"

"*Or* Pepthi," Natalia says. "Becauth it'th unhealthy!"

"Natalia, you have so," Katie-Rose says.

"Nope, not one thip."

"Bull-pooty," Katie-Rose says. "Everyone has had

60

Coke or Pepsi at some point. Even if you don't drink Coke now, I'm sure you had some when you were a baby, or at someone's birthday party. You just don't remember."

"Nope."

Katie-Rose turns to Yasaman. "She *has*."

Yasaman twists the end of her *hijab*. It's brown and gold, and makes her eyes appear even more luminous than usual. "We should go to class, or we'll get marked as tardy."

Natalia gestures at the police tape. "Are you going to leave that?"

"Yes," Katie-Rose says, because she certainly is now.

"What if you get in trouble?"

"Then I'll get in trouble. What's it to you?"

Yasaman's discomfort shimmers off her. "So I'll see you guys in Ms. Perez's room?" She waits less than half a second. "All right . . . well, bye!"

She quick-walks away. The hall is filling with other kids, but to Katie-Rose, it feels as if it's just her and Natalia. It also feels as if she's in an old-fashioned western shoot-out. She doesn't know how things got this bad this fast, but they did.

"When it comes to trans fats, I'm not afraid to put myself on the line," she tells Natalia. "But you want us to take the tape off the cabinet, 'cause you're scared of getting in trouble, so that's why you can't be part of our campaign."

Natalia presses her lips together. Her eyes somehow flatten out, too, and Katie-Rose yearns to call Yasaman back. If Yasaman could see Natalia now, she would see the real Natalia, the Natalia who is *not* sweet and innocent. But no, because if Yasaman came back, Natalia would slide back into her candy-coated shell. Katie-Rose shivers. It feels like a whisper on the nape of her neck.

"You're only thaying that to be mean," Natalia says. "I'm going to athk Yathaman, and Yathaman will thay yeth."

She spins on her heel.

"Wait!" Katie-Rose calls. Her heart beats fast. She wishes fleetingly that she had been nicer to Natalia from the beginning, but it's too late for that now.

Natalia pauses. She turns around.

"You can't ask Yasaman, because . . . because . . ."

"Becauth why, Katie-Rothe?"

Because I don't want you turning Yasaman against me, she wants to say, but she knows how babyish that would sound.

"Because I say so," she whispers.

Natalia smiles like Katie-Rose *is* a little baby. A silly little baby."Well, Katie-Rothe, that'th very interethting. There'th jutht one problem." She tilts her head. "It'th not up to you, ith it?"

Eight

A t ten fifteen, Mr. Emerson tells his students to line up for morning break, but unlike the others, Milla doesn't make a mad dash for the playground. She wants to stay a safe distance from Max, because she's nervous about seeing him after the embarrassed way she dashed out of Katie-Rose's house yesterday. Maybe he doesn't know about that. But what if he does?

She lingers by Mr. Emerson's desk. He's straightening his papers with one hand, because he only has one hand. Just one arm, too. He's cool, though.

"Is it all right if I go to the bathroom?" she asks.

"Of course, that's what break is for," he says. What he doesn't say—not in words—is, *And, Milla, did you really need to ask my permission?* Mr. Emerson wants Milla to work on being more independent. He told her moms so at back-to-school night.

"Do you want me to take the oar?" Milla asks. A kayak oar is Mr. Emerson's crazy version of a bathroom pass, but it's mainly for when kids need to go during class, not during break.

He gives her *the look,* which is the signal the two of them agreed on for the times when she's asking for too much teacher-approval. Mr. Emerson achieves *the look* by lowering his chin and pretending to peer over nonexistent glasses.

"I'll just leave it," Milla says.

"Excellent," Mr. Emerson replies.

She smiles to make sure he still likes her. He smiles back. Then he tells her to go on and let him do his work, please.

In the hall, Milla kicks her white sneakers against the floor. If she does it right, they squeak. Then she stops, because fifth graders probably aren't supposed to squeak, especially since the lower grades have already had their break and are back in class.

She goes into the girls' bathroom and stands there for a while, gazing at herself in the mirror. *Hello,* she tells herself silently. It's always a marvel to her that she is who she is. That she lives in this body. That she *is* this body. Everyone thinks she's pretty; she knows that. Sometimes she thinks she is, too. Other times, she sees herself more as combinations of color: blonde hair, blue eyes, rosebud lips. It's all so random, really.

She leaves the bathroom and wanders down the hall, peeking into various rooms. She spots Yasaman in the media center and goes over to her computer terminal. "Why aren't you outside?" she asks.

"I got a pass to stay inside," Yasaman says. She covers the screen with her hands. "I'm working on something for our website."

"What is it?" Milla asks.

"Just something. Stop looking!" Her eyes are bright, and Milla can see herself in them. In the bathroom mirror, her reflection was life-size. In Yasaman's eyes, she is tiny, tiny, but shiny.

Yasaman swivels in her chair to make Milla turn away from the computer. "Hey, thanks for leaving a comment on my blog last night. So what's your great Snack Attack idea?"

"If you're not telling, then neither am I," Milla says.

"Milla!"

The media center assistant rises from her desk.

"Kidding," Milla says. "I'll tell you at lunch, when we're all together. Bye!"

At last, she goes outside. She surveys the playground, and when she spots Max by the tetherball court, anxiety scurries up her and lodges in her rib cage. *Eeek!*

Next she searches for Katie-Rose and Violet. They're over by the swing set, and they seem to be staring at a boy named Cyril Remkiwicz, who's kind of a weirdie. Their heads are together, and they're whispering. As for Cyril, he's sitting on the rubber edge of a humongous tractor tire that serves as a sandbox for the younger kids. He's writing in the small spiral notebook he always has with him. His shirt has flying toasters on it.

Milla goes over.

"—but no one's ever seen inside it," Katie-Rose is

saying. She shifts her gaze. "Milla, hi. I'm telling Violet about Cyril."

Violet smiles at Milla. "Hey Mills. Cute top."

Milla looks down at her brown shirt with the white appliqué owl on it. She paired it with a denim miniskirt and brown boots that come halfway up her shins, because she wanted to look nice for Max.

"Thanks," she tells Violet.

"*Any*way," Katie-Rose continues. "We don't know for sure, but we think Cyril writes stuff down about people. Bad stuff. Right, Milla?"

Milla hesitates, because she feels guilty talking about people behind their backs. But that *is* the rumor. She nods.

"If no one's seen inside it, how do you know?" Violet asks. She's still new to Rivendell—she moved here from Atlanta—so there's tons she hasn't yet learned.

"Because if you *ask* him, he gives you his patented creepy eyeball look, and then he gets mad and writes down even more stuff," Katie-Rose explains. "About *you*."

Violet looks skeptical.

"Fine, I'll show you," Katie-Rose says. She raises her voice. "Hey! Cyril! What are you writing about?"

Cyril grows unnaturally still. Like, dead statue still.

"Cyril!" Katie-Rose calls again, as if there's the slightest chance he didn't hear her.

He lifts his head and shoots death rays at Katie-Rose. Then he hunches back over his notebook, scribbling furiously.

Katie-Rose shakes her head as if she's seen it all before. "The scowl-and-scribble. Did I tell you, or did I tell you?"

"You don't know it's about you," Violet points out.

"And he smells," Katie-Rose says.

"He does not," Milla protests, although sometimes he does.

"Oh, for cripe's sake!" Katie-Rose snaps. "Why is everybody jumping all over me today?"

Milla is confused. She looks helplessly at Violet, who turns to Katie-Rose and says, "What's going on? Who's jumping all over you?"

"Nothing. Never mind. Forget it." Katie-Rose pulls her eyebrows together. "He does have an *odor*, though. He takes a bath like once a week at the most."

Milla has no idea how often Cyril bathes and feels no

need to find out. She also doesn't understand why Katie-Rose is acting so irritable all of a sudden. She sneaks a peek at Max, who's much more pleasant to dwell on. He happens at the exact same moment to sneak a peek at her, and her heart flips over. *Eeek!*

She jerks her eyes back to Katie-Rose. She *glues* them there. Air is hitting parts of her eyeballs that aren't usually exposed to the elements, which makes her suspect her eyes are open too wide, but she can't make them go back to normal.

"Katie-Rose, don't be mean," she says, mainly to give the appearance of being smack in the middle of a conversation. She prays Max is no longer looking at her, and also that he is. With all that Max-ness going on, it takes her a moment to realize that Katie-Rose is close to tears.

Omigosh. Did she do that?

"Katie-Rose . . ." She touches her friend's arm. "Wait. You're not mean. You're one of the nicest people on the planet!"

"Not to everyone," Katie-Rose says.

"No one's nice to everyone," Violet says.

"Except Yasaman," Katie-Rose mutters. At least, that's what Milla *thinks* she says. Then Katie-Rose juts out her chin and raises her voice. "What smells worse than wet dog?" She supplies the answer herself. "Wet Cyril. And *I* didn't make that joke up. Modessa did."

Violet snorts. "Well, that *is* mean. Unsurprisingly."

"Yeah, and guess what?" Katie-Rose goes on. "There are other mean people at this school, too—and not just the ones you automatically think of."

Violet stares at Katie-Rose. So does Milla. Then Milla glances at Max, hoping he doesn't see Katie-Rose's red face and think that they're fighting. Milla would hate for him to think of her as a fighting type of girl.

"Well, you're not one of those other mean people," she tells Katie-Rose.

"I know," Katie-Rose says tightly.

"So! Um, let's talk about something happy!" Milla smiles. She subtly checks to see if Max notices, but not subtly enough, because when Milla turns back, there is mischief in Violet's eyes.

Violet slings her arm around Milla. "Milla?" she says. "I think we should take a walk."

"Why Milla and not me?" Katie-Rose says.

"Because we're going to go talk to Max. Right, Milla?"

Milla opens her mouth, but she has no words. When it comes to mixed-sex conversations, she is more the proceed-with-extreme-caution type, if she proceeds at all.

"*Ohhhhh,*" Katie-Rose says.

"Chop-chop," Violet says briskly, and Milla tries not to hyperventilate. Her mind turns fleetingly to her mom's friend's lake house, which has a dock leading to the cold lake water. One day she jumped off, just to prove she could, and the memory of that moment washes over her. She's once more in the air, knowing that the cold water will swallow her up, and that it will be terrible and wonderful, both.

Nine

Violet

At the tetherball court, Max swats the ball to his best friend, Thomas. Two yards away, Milla grabs Violet's arm to keep Violet from going closer.

"I can't!" she whispers. "What would I *say*?"

"How about, 'Hey there, hot stuff. How's the old tetherball treating you?'" Violet suggests.

Milla swats her. "Violet! I am *not* calling him 'hot stuff'!"

"All right, I will," Violet says. There are certain things Violet is wimpy about (Exhibit A: Visiting Her Mom), but in most situations, she's pretty fearless. And as for Max, there is nothing the slightest bit scary about this solid, good-natured boy who likes hamsters and dominoes and tetherball.

She marches over. "Hi, hot stuff."

"Violet!" Milla gasps. She joins them, her face turning the color of a cherry tomato.

"You did *not* just say that," she says to Violet. She turns to Max. "She did *not* just say that, I swear."

Max is confused. "Say what?"

"*Hot stuff,*" Violet whispers in Milla's ear. Milla stomps on her foot, giggling all the while.

"She said 'hi,' and that is all," Milla tells Max. She lifts her own hand halfway. "Um. Hi!"

Max smiles. Then the tetherball swings around the pole and whacks his face.

"Ow." He steps back. *"Ow."*

"Dude, are you okay?" Thomas says.

"Omigosh," Milla cries. She raises her hand to the red mark rising on his skin. She touches it with the very barest tips of her fingers.

"Want me to get an ice pack?" Thomas says.

"No," Max says, dazed. He makes his way to a metal picnic table. "But seriously, *ow*. Owwie ow ow."

Aw, Violet thinks. It's pretty adorkable for a boy to say *owwie ow ow*, but Violet can get behind adorkable, especially when it comes to Milla. Milla could have the studliest, slickest, jerkiest boy in the grade if she wanted. Adorkable is much better.

"I got stung by a bee once," Milla says, holding Max's elbow and helping him sit down. "Not on my cheek. On my ear. On my ear*lobe*, actually."

Thomas laughs. Violet glares at him.

"And, um ..." Milla glances from face to face as if she's forgotten where she was going with this. "Um ..."

"Was it owwie ow ow?" Max says.

"Yes!" Milla says, her face brightening with relief. "My earlobe swelled up and turned purple. It was like a really ugly earring."

Happiness settles over Violet. She likes Max for saying *owwie ow ow*, and she likes him even more for saving Milla when he saw she needed saving. She's proud of herself for bringing the two of them together, even if it did mean that Max got clubbed by the tetherball.

"I don't get why girls wear earrings," Thomas says. "Why would you want to poke a *hole* in yourself?"

"My ears aren't pierced yet," Milla says. "My moms say I have to wait till I'm eleven, which at least is one year earlier than Yasaman, who has to wait till she's twelve."

Violet fingers her own ear, which is adorned with a dangling daisy. Her ears have been pierced since she was four weeks old.

"I always wanted a baby girl," her mom used to tell her, "and I always knew I'd pierce her ears. I think baby girls are so precious with pierced ears, don't you?" Then she'd give Violet a hug. "And you were the most precious baby ever. You're still precious, even though—I know, I know—you're a big girl now. But you'll always be my baby . . . and that makes me the luckiest mama ever."

Does she miss me? Violet wonders. *Does she know how much I miss her?*

Her mean voice chimes in: *How could she? She probably thinks you've forgotten her.*

Violet puts her hand on her stomach, because something's gnawing at her from within. A small animal, maybe a hamster. *Gross.* Sometimes Violet's thoughts are so strange they scare her.

She shakes her head to clear it and latches onto Max's words, stringing them into a rope strong enough to hold her.

"But we stopped at the pet store," Max is saying, "because it's next to the gym where my mom works out. And one of the mama hamsters had a litter of babies, and they were old enough not to need her anymore."

Not to need their mother anymore? Violet thinks. *The cramping returns.*

No. Focus. Sometimes a baby hamster is just a baby hamster—and anyway, look how well Milla is handling this. Hamsters freak Milla out, but is she letting that stop her? If Milla can rise to the occasion, so can Violet.

"And I looked at Stewy, and I knew he was the one," Max finishes.

"It was meant to be," Milla says.

"That was so nice of your mom to let you get him," Violet says.

"Yeah, but she said about a thousand times that it was *my* job to take care of him. Like to make sure he's always got food and water, and clean out his cage, and not let him die."

Thomas chortles. "Did she say those actual words? 'Don't let him die'?"

Max blushes. "Well, she had two mice when she was little, and they died. Their names were Heidi and Holly. I guess she forgot to feed them for, like, a really long time, and ... yeah."

"That's *terrible!*" Milla says, and Violet isn't surprised when her eyes well up.

Milla's like that when it comes to animals. Even rodents, apparently. Even *insects*. Last week, Milla practically burst into tears after Katie-Rose killed a fruit fly that flew out of her lunch bag as the girls were unpacking their food. Katie-Rose did it instinctively and not to be a murderer or anything. She saw the fruit fly and slapped her hands together. Then she unfolded her hands and showed the remains to the other FFFs, saying "Ew."

"Oh, poor thing," Milla cried. "Is it dead? For sure dead?"

Katie-Rose regarded the smushed-ness. She looked up at Milla like, *Oops?*

"It's a fruit fly," Violet told Milla. "It would have died soon anyway."

"True," Katie-Rose said. "Fruit flies have very short life spans. Anyway, I didn't mean to."

"I know," Milla said. "It's just so sad. Its life was already doomed to be short, and ... well ... now it's not just short, it's *over*. I know you didn't mean to, Katie-Rose, but it's just so tragic!"

It took Yasaman to calm her down. She gave Katie-Rose a napkin to wipe her hands with and said to Milla, "Maybe it was wounded already. Maybe Katie-Rose eased its suffering."

Katie-Rose liked this idea. "Yeah! It was trapped all day with my apple and my juice box—I bet it got pretty banged up in there. I'm sure it did! *I* think I'm probably an angel of mercy, Milla."

"Saint Katie-Rose," Violet said, totally deadpan. Everyone except Milla had laughed, but Milla had *almost* laughed.

Thomas has launched into a story of a goldfish with an infected scale, but Violet can already predict the ending—dead mice, dead fruit fly, dead fish—and she doesn't want to hear it. She glances around the playground to see what else is going on.

Katie-Rose is swinging with a girl named Ava. Mr. Emerson is telling Ms. Perez a story, and Ms. Perez laughs. She looks flushed and pretty. By the giant tire, Cyril is still writing away in that notebook of his, only—

Huh. He seems to have company: Modessa and her evil twin, Quin. They're not *really* twins. They're both equally vile, that's all. And that's putting it nicely.

As Violet watches, Quin darts forward, pokes Cyril, and darts back to Modessa. The two of them snicker when Cyril startles, but when he looks at them, they switch immediately to *la la la, I didn't notice anything just now, did you?*

Anger flashes in Cyril's eyes, along with something else, something that shouldn't be seen. Like the purply guts of the mice Violet's neighbor's cat used to leave on Violet's doorstep. The cat brought them as presents, but sometimes the mice weren't always all the way dead, and those inside bits . . .

Nobody's inside bits should be exposed like that, and especially not without permission.

Cyril hunches back over his notebook. Quin deer-hops forward and pokes him, and Cyril flinches. "Hey!" he says. "Quit it!"

Modessa claps and doubles over, and Quin's chest puffs out with pride at pleasing Queen Modessa. Violet wants to vomit.

Just because Cyril is different, does that mean Quin's allowed to poke him? *No.*

Just because he smells—if he even does—does that give Modessa the right to make jokes about him? *No.*

Violet's mom sometimes forgot to shower, back when signs of her illness were just starting to show up. Sometimes she went weeks without clipping her toenails, remembering their existence only when her shoes pressed them painfully into her flesh. She'd rub the blisters, and Violet would say, "Mom, it's your toenails. You need to cut them so they don't do that."

Violet's own toes curl inside her baby-doll shoes. Then she uncurls them and heads over to give Quin and Modessa a piece of her mind.

"Violet?" Milla says.

Violet flutters her hand over her shoulder to say,

Keep talking to Max, you're doing great. Don't mind me. She gets close enough to Quin and Modessa that she can make out their words.

"...worth fifty points," Modessa is saying. "But only if you touch his head."

"Ew!" Quin squeals. "That's worth a hundred points at least."

"Fine, a hundred points. If you bring back a hair."

"*Ewwww!* No way am I touching his greasy hair!"

"Good, I'm glad we agree," Violet says.

Modessa and Quin spin around. Quin's mouth falls open, and even Modessa turns a little pink.

"You're being jerks," Violet says. "Why do you keep poking him like it's some sort of game?"

Modessa recovers first. "Because it *is* a game. It's called Poke the Psycho."

Well. That was the wrong thing to say.

"Leave him alone," Violet warns.

Modessa touches her chin and stares at the sky. Then she drops her finger and says, "Um ... nah." She turns to Quin. "Quin? A hundred points?"

Quin steps toward Cyril, but Violet grabs her wrist.

"What's your problem?" Quin says. She tries to twist free. "Let go!"

"No," Violet says. She glances at Cyril, expecting him to help her out. Or if not that, expecting him to at least look grateful.

But, no. His eyes are dark and stormy, and his jaw is set at an ugly angle. He glares at all of them, Modessa, Quin, *and* Violet, before curving over his notebook and unleashing a torrent of cramped words.

Whiteness—too bright—flares in Violet's brain. Quin squirms free.

"Poke him," Modessa commands. "I'll give you *five* hundred points."

Quin snickers and strides toward Cyril. Violet feels physically ill. She steps backward and bumps smack into Mr. Emerson, who has appeared without her noticing.

He steadies her. To Modessa and Quin, he says, "Girls, I'm appalled. I want you to apologize to Cyril *now.*"

Quin grows pale, and Modessa immediately loses her smirk. Relief courses through Violet's veins. Order *is* possible. Violet *isn't* crazy for sticking up for Cyril.

"Sorry," Quin mutters.

Cyril doesn't respond.

"Modessa?" Mr. Emerson prods.

Modessa pretends to be confused. She looks at Mr. Emerson from under her eyelashes and says, "I don't understand what I'm supposed to apologize for. Is joking around not allowed anymore?"

"Poking someone isn't a joke," Mr. Emerson says.

"But . . . Quin pokes me all the time, and I poke her, too," Modessa says. "It's a game. Right, Quin?"

Quin fidgets, until Modessa slips her hand into Quin's. Then Quin grows still. She nods.

"Does Cyril know it's a game?" Mr. Emerson says.

"Of course!" Modessa says, sounding wounded. She turns to Cyril and slathers on the charm. "You know we're just playing, right, Cyril?"

Violet is disgusted, but she's pretty sure Mr. Emerson sees through Modessa's act, and she's positive Cyril does. *Go on,* she coaches him silently. *Tell him the truth.*

But Cyril says nothing. His face is expressionless.

"Cyril?" Mr. Emerson says.

Time stretches out. The playground blurs. Cyril isn't

going to defend himself, and Modessa isn't going to apologize. Order isn't order after all.

Mr. Emerson keeps talking. Modessa keeps being Modessa. Violet pulls numbly inside of herself, until Mr. Emerson's tone changes, bringing her back.

"Cyril, wait," he says. He raises his voice. *"Cyril!"*

Violet blinks. Cyril is gone.

Ten

So Modessa never did apologize?" Yasaman asks during lunch. Violet has shared the dark tale of the Cyril-poking game, and Yasaman is struggling to wrap her head around it. How can someone not apologize when she (a) *needs* to apologize, and (b) has even been ordered by her teacher to apologize?

"Where is she now?" Milla asks, looking around the lunchroom.

"Hiding out, probably," Katie-Rose says. "She probably came up with some fake help-a-teacher job she absolutely *had* to do." She doesn't make eye contact with Yasaman. She hasn't since they sat down, which is not very Katie-Rose-like. Is it possible Katie-Rose is ignoring her because of what happened this morning, with Natalia and the police tape?

"Maybe she's helping Angie organize the bookshelves," Yasaman says.

"Helping Angie eat cookies, you mean," Katie-Rose says bitterly.

Angie, the parent volunteer who's in charge of Rivendell's small media center, is famous for her cookies. She brings them to her student mentors every Monday. Katie-Rose wanted to be a media center mentor, but she wasn't selected. Modessa was.

"Well, she'll have to come out eventually," Violet says. She's still angry, but her voice is strong and assured. "When she does, Mr. Emerson will find her, and he'll *make* her apologize. End of story."

Yasaman drops her eyes. Milla fidgets, and Katie-Rose exhales through her nose in her bull-snort-ish way.

"What?" Violet says.

No one responds.

Violet shakes the table, and a little bit of milk sloshes out of Yasaman's carton. Violet winces. "*Ack.* Sorry, Yaz."

"It's okay," Yasaman says.

"But for real. What are y'all not telling me?"

Milla shifts uncomfortably, and Yasaman can guess what she's thinking: that she's the one who should explain, since she's the one who used to be friends with Modessa. She picks up her fork and turns it over in her hands. She says, "She's done this before, that's all."

Violet frowns.

"Um, not to Cyril, but to Elena."

"Who's Elena?" Violet asks.

"She's in Ms. Perez's class with me and Yasaman," Katie-Rose says.

"She lives on a tiny little farm outside of town," Yasaman contributes. "Out past the highway, where all that open space is."

"Her parents raise llamas," Milla says. "They sell the wool to people. And Modessa—"

"Last year, she called Elena 'Llama Girl,'" Katie-Rose says. "Whenever Elena came around, she'd sniff the air and say things like, 'Does anyone smell llama poop?'"

"Doesn't Elena have a pig, too?" Milla muses. "Like, as a pet?"

"Oh yeah," Katie-Rose says. "Modessa made oinking sounds, too."

Violet shakes her head. "Wow, how original. Didn't she get in trouble?"

"Kind of," Yasaman says. "Elena told on her, and Modessa was *supposed* to apologize, but she never did."

"But that's just wrong," Violet states.

"I know," Yasaman says.

"You can't just . . ." Violet puts down her sandwich. "Just because *someone's* different . . ."

"Tell it to the police," Katie-Rose says darkly. "Modessa never apologized to Elena, and I swear to you, she'll never apologize to Cyril, either. If she does, I will first laugh in amazement, and then fall over dead in a faint, and there will be little *x*'s where my eyes should be."

Violet looks stunned. She looks like someone just stole her lollipop, and not at all like the strong, tough Violet Yasaman's used to.

Yasaman decides to change the subject. "Um, speaking of farms . . ."

"Who's speaking of farms?" Katie-Rose interrupts. "I'm not speaking about farms."

"Elena's farm," Milla says.

Katie-Rose makes a *plfff* sound.

Yasaman falters, then says, "I think it's cool, that's all. That her family lives on a real farm, tiny or not. Do you know what I mean?"

"As opposed to a tiny fake farm?" Katie-Rose says.

"Actually, yes. I did some research on the company that makes Cheezy D'lites, and they pretend to be a farm, but they're not."

Milla tilts her head. "Meaning what?"

"The company's name is Happy Healthy Farms," Yasaman tells her. "And that makes you think of, like, a happy farm with grass and cows and puffy white clouds, right?"

"I guess," Milla says.

"But it's a factory," Yasaman says. "There's *no farm*. There are no farmers. There are no puffy clouds."

"Are there cows?" Katie-Rose asks.

"Yes, but they live in a stockyard. Oh, and get this: Cheezy D'lites have *no cheese* in them at all. Not one single ounce of cheese."

"Then what are the cows for?" Katie-Rose asks.

"Because they make other things besides Cheezy D'lites. Like frozen cheeseburgers, which maybe have real cheese in them or maybe don't, I'm not sure. But the hamburger part is cow."

"Gross," Violet says.

"I know," Yasaman says. "Which is why, you know . . . the Snack Attack! Did you guys read my blog entry last night?"

"You know I did, because I left a comment," Milla says.

"Wait," Violet says. "If they're called Cheezy D'lites, but they have no cheese in them . . ." She shakes her head. "They should be called *Non*–Cheezy D'lites, and the Happy Healthy people should be called Stupid Unhealthy Liars. Omigosh, I *hate* people like that. It's like Modessa all over again! It's the exact same thing!"

"It is?" Yasaman says.

Violet presses her hands on the table and leans forward. "Modessa thinks she's above the rules of the school, like they don't even apply to her. Right?"

"They pretty much don't," Katie-Rose mutters.

"And why? Because when teachers come around, she fools them into thinking she's a pretty perfect princess. But she's not. She's a total phony, just like those Happy Healthy stupid-heads!"

Yasaman furrows her brow. Yes, Modessa and Quin are phony, and yes, Cheezy D'lites are a big fake. Which is why Yasaman wants to get rid of them!

But the whole world is fake-ish, to a degree. Like how Yasaman tells her aunt how good her fried liver is, when it's not actually to her liking. Or when a teacher says, "Good morning, Yasaman. How are you today?" and Yasaman says "fine," even if she's not. Everyone does that. No one ever says, "Well, frankly, my elbow hurts, and I don't know why. Oh, and I'm wearing the same socks I wore yesterday. It's *possible* my feet might be stinky."

"Everybody lies sometimes," Yasaman says.

"Not my mom," Violet mutters.

Everyone falls silent, because Violet hardly ever talks about her mom.

"She doesn't know how," Violet goes on. Adopting a strong Southern accent, she says, "'Oh, Lavinia, the bake sale is coming up, and it would be *fabulous* if you could whip up a dozen or so *pot du crème*s. You *do* have a good recipe for *pot du crème,* don't you?'" She goes back to her normal voice. "No, and who cares?!"

Yasaman isn't sure, but she guesses Violet is mimicking the fancy ladies Violet's mother had to be around at Violet's old school in Atlanta. Yasaman herself has never heard of a *pot du crème.*

Ohhhh, Yasaman thinks, figuring something out. Maybe one reason Violet is so worked up about Modessa and Quin is because they're like the kid versions of the *pot du crème* lady. Phony and fake, and using that phony-fakeness to make other people feel bad.

It is Milla who breaks the tension by saying, "So we'll *fight* the phoniness. That's what my comment was about, on Yaz's blog." She glances from friend to friend. "Don't you want to know what my secret Snack Attack weapon is?"

"Totally," Yasaman says. "Tell us!"

Milla grins impishly. She ducks under the table, unzips her backpack, and emerges with a brown plastic bottle. "Voilà!"

"Me no understand," Violet says.

"They're Jelly-Yums," Milla says. "Mom Joyce got them as a party favor at Sara's blessing way."

Katie-Rose reaches across the table and takes the bottle. "Why's there a picture of a giraffe on the label?"

"I have no idea, but two Jelly-Yums equal one whole serving of fruits and vegetables," Milla says. "Instant healthiness!"

Katie-Rose unscrews the lid and peers inside. "*Pew!* They stink!"

She shoves the jar at Yasaman, who shakes a handful of the Jelly-Yums into her palm. They resemble jelly beans, except they're swampy colored. And they do smell pretty gross.

"Try one," Milla urges.

"Um, sure," Yasaman says. "Okay." She passes them out, only Katie-Rose refuses to accept hers, so Yasaman places it by her sandwich. Katie-Rose eyes it antagonistically, and Milla sighs.

"You just have to eat it quickly, that's all. There *is* a slight weird flavor at the very beginning, but then it goes away." She puts hers in her mouth, chews, and swallows. "See?"

Yasaman goes for it. Her eyes water as the taste hits her, and she gags, but she gets it down. "Not bad," she manages to say.

"And now you've had a full serving of fruit and veggies!" Milla exclaims.

"Half a serving," Katie-Rose corrects. "You said she had to eat two."

"I can do that," Yasaman says bravely. She reaches for Katie-Rose's, but Katie-Rose slaps her hand.

"Keep yer paws off my bean," she growls. "I *might* eat it one day."

"When you're thirty?" Violet asks. "Hey, can I see the jar?"

Milla passes it over, and Violet reads aloud the list of ingredients. "Blueberry, raspberry, pomegranate." She makes a face. *"Beets?"*

"Beets aren't bad," Yasaman says.

"Yes, they are," Katie-Rose says.

"Broccoli," Violet says. "Wow. And kale. And spirulina, whatever that is."

"No clue," Milla says.

Violet pops her bean into her mouth. A range of expressions play over her face: first *yuck*, then *meh*, then *well, look at that, I seem to have survived.*

"I feel healthier already," she proclaims. She holds out her hand. "Hit me again. I want my full serving of spiru-whatever."

Yasaman smiles. She's happy that Violet likes the Jelly-Yums (or, perhaps more accurately, is willing to eat the Jelly-Yums), and she's happy that Milla brought them in the first place. The Snack Attack is off to an excellent start.

And then Natalia appears at their table. "Hey, girlth," she says.

Katie-Rose's fingers close over her bean. Her face closes down, too, and Yasaman's stomach sinks. Katie-Rose was so rude to Natalia this morning, and now here she is doing it again. Which means, again, that Yasaman will have to be doubly nice to make up for it.

"Hi, Natalia," she says weakly.

"What'th up?" Natalia asks. She glances at the Jelly-Yums bottle. "What'cha got there?"

"Nothing," Katie-Rose says.

"We're working on our Snack Attack campaign," Yasaman says. "Milla brought us these vitamin things, and ... yeah." She pauses. "Do you, um, want one?"

She shakes out one of the Jelly-Yums and offers it to Natalia. *Eau de* spirulina rises in a cloud.

Natalia steps back. "Oh. No, thankth."

"Why not?" Katie-Rose challenges.

"Becauth I don't need a vitamin. I already eat healthy."

"I'm sure you don't *always*," Katie-Rose says. "You eat junk food, too, and don't even try to lie this time, because I've seen you. I've seen you eating Green Apple Sour Loops, and the reason I remember is because I like them, too!"

Yasaman wants to groan. If Katie-Rose wants Natalia to leave, then she shouldn't engage in a conversation with her about Green Apple Sour Loops. She shouldn't engage with her, period.

But, no. Katie-Rose puts her own bean in her mouth and chews vigorously. "Mmm, delicious. Delicious *and* nutritious." She plucks the unclaimed Jelly-Yum from Yasaman's palm and eats it, too. Then she grabs the whole bottle and spills five or six of the swampy beans straight into her open mouth. She makes exaggerated sounds of pleasure as she works away at them.

"That'th dithguthting, and no, I do *not* like Green Apple Thour Loopth," Natalia says. "If you thaw thome-one eating them, it wathn't me." She turns to Yasaman. "But I *would* like to help with the Thnack Attack."

Yasaman feels Katie-Rose glowering, but her mouth is full of Jelly-Yums, and she can't speak.

"Um, I guess," Yasaman says.

"Fabulouth," Natalia says. "I have a button maker at home. Want me to make buttonth?"

Something is drumming a beat into Yasaman's shin. Something named Katie-Rose's foot. But what is Yasaman supposed to do? She can't hurt Natalia's feelings.

"Sure," she says helplessly.

Katie-Rose groans and throws herself back in her seat. Milla and Violet don't look pleased, either.

Natalia claps and says, "Oh yay! Thith ith going to be thuch fun, don't you think?"

Yasaman is upset with Natalia for putting her in this position, and she's upset with her friends for not understanding that she didn't *want* to include Natalia in their campaign.

She's beginning to see how people get sucked into acting fake. More than that, she's beginning to see how nearly impossible it is to stay real.

Eleven

Katie-Rose's stomach cramps painfully as Mrs. Gunderson, the music teacher, explains to Chance for the forty-fourth time that there's no need to blow so hard on his recorder.

"You are not lost in the forest, blowing your safety whistle as if your life depends on it," she says.

Everyone laughs except Katie-Rose, who hunches over her desk. It's those cursed Jelly-Yums. They're rolling around in her gut, releasing beet gas and broccoli gas and spirulina gas, whatever spirulina is. And all that gas is building and roiling and—

Owwww. It's not good. It's very bad, in fact. Very *very* bad. She waits for the spasm to pass, then rises from her desk and tries to walk normally to her music teacher's desk.

"May I please have the bathroom pass?" she whispers.

"Katie-Rose, you just came from lunch," Mrs. Gunderson chides. "You're supposed to use that time to make your bathroom trips."

It's true, possibly, that Katie-Rose has a history of making more trips to the bathroom than the average fifth grader, but that's because she gets squirmy sometimes, especially during music. Especially when they're playing their recorders. She's failed her "Mary Had a Little Lamb" test three times now.

But this isn't one of her squirmy times. Well, *yes* squirmy—horribly, dangerously squirmy—but not ag-I-hate-my-recorder squirmy. If she doesn't get to the bathroom soon . . .

Mrs. Gunderson must read this in Katie-Rose's eyes, because she sighs and hands Katie-Rose the pass.

After a l-o-n-g stay in her favorite stall, Katie-Rose feels better. *But no more Jelly-Yums,* she tells herself.

Jelly-Yums are not snacktastic. Jelly-Yums are the devil's candy.

The Snack Attack itself must go on, however. They just need to find a new healthy Cheezy D'lites replacement, and with*out* any help from Natalia. Stupid Natalia, worming her way in where she's not wanted and most definitely not needed. Katie-Rose makes a detour on her way back to music, hoping a peek at the taped-shut snack cabinet will cheer her up.

Only when she gets there—*aaaargh!*

That stupid, annoying, meddlesome Natalia!

Fuming, Katie-Rose tugs her Sony Cybershot out of her jeans pocket, extends her arm, and aims the video camera at herself.

FADE IN:

INTERIOR RIVENDELL ELEMENTARY—HALLWAY BY THE SNACK CABINET—MORNING

Behind Katie-Rose's scowling face is the snack cabinet, cleared of *all* black-and-yellow police tape.

KATIE-ROSE

Natalia took down the tape! Do you see now, Yasaman? Do you see how Natalia is *not* someone who should be part of the Snack Attack? She took down private property just to make me mad, and let me tell you, it worked. And let me also tell you something about Natalia. Natalia is ... She's just plain ...

Katie-Rose's lips poof out as she struggles to come up with the right words.

KATIE-ROSE (CONT'D)

She's worse than trans fats ... worse, even, than cheez pretending to be cheese! Because you don't know this, but she is buddying up to you and then turning around and being *ha ha* and braggy to me about how you're *her* friend now. Did you know that?

Off-screen, someone clears her throat. Not a kid. A grown-up.

KATIE-ROSE (CONT'D)

(pasting on a nervous smile)

Uh . . . hi there.

Katie-Rose rotates her camera 180 degrees. Her teacher Ms. Perez fills the frame.

MS. PEREZ

(amused)

Hi there yourself. And no, I didn't know that. Care to enlighten me?

KATIE-ROSE (off-screen)

Um. Someone stole my private property. Can you punish her?

MS. PEREZ

So *you're* the one who taped shut the cabinet. Is that what you mean by "private property"? The police tape?

Katie-Rose's expression can't be seen. If it could, it would be classic *oops*.

KATIE-ROSE (off-screen)

Uh... uh...

Ms. Perez waits. She's young and fun, and Katie-Rose has always wondered why she isn't married. Sometimes the fifth-grade girls talk about it, and some of them say it's because she's too chubby. Katie-Rose thinks that's ridiculous. Today Ms. Perez is wearing a flowery blouse with fluffy ruffles cascading down the front. She looks pretty.

MS. PEREZ

Katie-Rose, are you filming me?

KATIE-ROSE (off-screen)

Maybe? You're very photogenic. Have you ever considered a career in Hollywood?

Ms. Perez laughs.

MS. PEREZ

Thank you, Katie-Rose, but I'm quite happy being a teacher. Were you hoping I might pack up and move? Maybe right this very second?

KATIE-ROSE (off-screen)

Ha ha. No. Ha ha.

MS. PEREZ

Sweetie, do you want to put the camera down so I can see your face?

KATIE-ROSE (off-screen)

No thanks. But thanks for the offer.

MS. PEREZ

Do you want to tell me why you taped shut the snack cabinet?

KATIE-ROSE (off-screen)

Uh, no thanks, but thanks for the—

MS. PEREZ

(interrupting)

I'm the one who took the tape off, by the way. And let me rephrase: Katie-Rose, why did you tape shut the snack cabinet?

Off-screen, Katie-Rose exhales. Another rumor about Ms. Perez is that she's better with kids than with adults, and that's why she can't find a husband. But Katie-Rose doesn't think she's being all that great with kids right now.

It would be much better if Ms. Perez just walked away and forgot this little incident ever happened. But she doesn't. Her expression stays pleasant, but it's clear she expects an answer.

KATIE-ROSE (off-screen)

Because we're protesting the Cheezy D'lites we have for morning snack. Because of trans fats and cheez that isn't cheese. Do you know how bad that stuff is?

Ms. Perez glances ruefully at her figure.

                    MS. PEREZ
Well, yes.

                    KATIE-ROSE
                (building momentum)
Then you understand where we're coming from!
We are the hope of the future, Ms. Perez! Do you
really want your very own students stuffed to
the gills with partially hydro—
                (stumbling over the word)
—hydrogenated curtain seed and/or soybean
oil? *Do* you?

                    MS. PEREZ
I think you mean *cottonseed* oil. Not curtain
seed.

                KATIE-ROSE (off-screen)
Did I say "curtain seed oil"?

MS. PEREZ

You did.

KATIE-ROSE (off-screen)

(giggling)

Curtain seed oil. That's funny.

Ms. Perez giggles, too. Then she catches herself and straightens her shoulders. She reaches out and *makes* Katie-Rose lower her camera. For a moment, there is the pinkish blur of Ms. Perez's hand, and then the screen shows Ms. Perez's flats, which are fabulous and purple, as well as Katie-Rose's sneakers, which she has doodled on with a pen. The audio function continues to capture their conversation.

MS. PEREZ (off-screen)

Katie-Rose, I will take your snack concerns under consideration. All right?

KATIE-ROSE (off-screen)

You will?

MS. PEREZ (off-screen)

I'm not the one who places the snack orders,
and my suspicion is that it comes down to the
fact that Cheezy D'lites are the least expensive
option. So there may not be anything I can do
about it. Though you can certainly choose not
to eat yours.

KATIE-ROSE (off-screen)

Well, I don't know about that. A girl's got to eat,
you know.

MS. PEREZ (off-screen)

But if you wanted to give a presentation about
nutrition to the class, I would say "yes" to that.

KATIE-ROSE (off-screen)

(happily)

That would be awesome! Could I give my presentation to Mr. Emerson's class, too? And Mr.
Emerson is cute, by the way. Don't you think?

MS. PEREZ (off-screen)

What?

KATIE-ROSE (off-screen)

I think you two should go out—unless you already have a boyfriend. Do you?

Ms. Perez steps backward, her purple flats toeing inward.

MS. PEREZ (off-screen)

Katie-Rose, this is not . . . an appropriate topic. And, just as a life lesson, it's never a good idea to date someone you work with.

KATIE-ROSE (off-screen)

How come?

MS. PEREZ (off-screen)
(sounding flustered)

Okay, I think we're done here. And let's keep your presentation specific to our class. I think that's best, don't you?

KATIE-ROSE (off-screen)

Well, actually—

MS. PEREZ (off-screen)

(interrupting)

Katie-Rose? Go to class.

KATIE-ROSE (off-screen)

But I'm having such a good time chatting with you! Anyway, all we're doing in music is practicing our recorders, and believe me, becoming a master recorder player is not what I—

MS. PEREZ (off-screen)

(sternly)

Now. And why don't you hand me your camera for safekeeping if you're not going to put it away?

The image of Katie-Rose's sneakers wobbles.

KATIE-ROSE (off-screen)

I'm putting it away, see? Here I am, putting it

away, and then fine, I'll head back to music if you insist. Although I promise you, what the world needs now is *not*—

MS. PEREZ (off-screen)

Why don't you go on and give it to me, hmm?

KATIE-ROSE (off-screen)

Oh, no. No need. But thanks for the offer! Bye!

FADE TO BLACK

Twelve

Camilla

That evening, Milla decides to write a blog entry. She's never written a blog entry before, but then, she's never gone up to Max on the playground before, either. And look how well that went! She shakes her hips, throws her arms wide, and belts out a single, pop star–esque *"Laaaaa!"* Then she flops down on her bed and grabs her laptop. She goes to LuvYaBunches.com.

Post an entry? it says at the top of the blog page.

"Why, yes," Milla replies. She selects her trademark font and names her entry: Doodly-doodly-doo!

She pauses. *Hmm.* "Doodly-doodly-doo" does not

a blog entry make, but she gets writer's block all of a sudden. She knows what she wants to write about—Max!—but the prospect of typing out words and seeing them on the screen and having them be real . . .

It makes her heart squeak.

She could hit Exit, and no one would be the wiser. She doesn't *have* to write a blog entry. It's totally up to her. But she wants to, so she centers her hands over the keyboard and forbids herself from overthinking. *Just go for it*, she commands herself.

Blog

I am happy! Yay! And I like being happy and want to stay this way forever! 😊😊😊😊😊😊

I'm happy cuz I lurve my friends and I lurve my family and I lurve Rivendell. I lurve *almost* every single person in the fifth grade, especially ppl who are nice and have hamsters. And—hold on to your chair—I *MIGHT* EVEN LURVE HAMSTERS. Shocker! I know!!!!!

But maybe I was being unfair to hamsters. Maybe I should get to know an actual hamster and *then* decide. But it has to be a cute hamster who has a cute owner named Stewy.

Um, the *hamster* has to be named Stewy. Not the owner. Hee hee. 🤭

Milla tilts her head. She's happy, she maybe likes hamsters (because if Max likes them, they can't be all bad, right?), and she definitely likes Max. That's really all she wanted to say, and now she's said it, even if she didn't use Max's actual name. Can a blog entry be just ... that?

The *brring-brring* of the telephone interrupts her thoughts. When Mom Abigail calls out that it's for her, she thinks, *Well, there ya go. Guess a blog entry can be just that.* She clicks Save, feeling proud of herself for having done something new and slightly scary.

Downstairs, she grabs the phone from the counter and walks with it to the brown suede sofa in front of the TV. This level of their house consists primarily of one huge space called the great room, which includes the kitchen (where Mom Abigail is making brownies, *mmm*), an eating area, and a lounging-about area. Milla drapes herself over the arm of the sofa and brings the phone to her ear.

"Hello?"

"Hi, this is Max," Max says, and Milla bolts back up as if her spine is spring-loaded.

"I know," Milla says, because she recognizes his voice. Her heart whomps in her rib cage, and she glances at Mom Abigail. She appears busy with her brownie batter, which is good, because who needs her mom listening in on an opposite-sex conversation? "I mean—hi!"

"Hi," Max says for the second time.

"Hi," she replies. What will she do if they go on like this forever? *Hi. Hi. Hi. Hi? Hi!* From the corner of her eye, she sees Mom Abigail looking at her, and she climbs over the arm of the sofa and scooches way down into the cushions.

"Do you want to come over tomorrow?" Max says in a rush. "To meet Stewy? Since you didn't get to on Sunday."

Milla's thoughts race. So does her pulse. Does he mean just her, or her and Katie-Rose? Because Katie-Rose lives right next door. Or maybe, just maybe, he means Milla all by herself? Since Katie-Rose already met Stewy?

Oh dear. She has to say something, so she says, "You mean with Katie-Rose? Like that she and I could come over after school, is that what you mean?"

Max hesitates. "Um, sure, I guess."

Ag! If Milla could, she would bonk herself over the head with a frying pan, because he *did* mean just her. *Bonk, bonk, bonk.* But since she is without a frying pan, the least she can do is try again.

"Or, well, how about if I come over by myself?" she says. "Not that Katie-Rose couldn't come over, too, like if she randomly said to herself, *Oh, I think I'll go to Max's house.* But she wouldn't *have* to, necessarily."

"Yeah," Max says. His voice is brighter. "She probably won't, but if she does, I won't slam the door in her face or anything."

She giggles. "Good."

"Hi, Katie-Rose!" Max says, acting out what he wouldn't do. *"SLAM!"*

"That would be so mean! Or what if she was a Girl Scout, selling cookies?"

"Hi, little Girl Scout," Max says. He raises his voice. "NO, I DON'T WANT ANY COOKIES!"

"Slam!" Milla says. A smile stretches across her face, and she stops feeling quite so nervous. And, of course, they would never *really* slam the door on Katie-Rose.

"My mom wanted me to be a Girl Scout," Max confesses.

Milla's eyebrows swoop up. "What?!"

"I know. Don't tell anyone."

"Wait. Why would she want you to be a *Girl* Scout?"

"A Girl Scout?" Mom Abigail says. "Max wants to be a Girl Scout?"

Milla pushes herself up so she can see over the sofa. Covering the mouthpiece of the phone, she says, "Mo-o-o-om!"

"Sorry, sorry," Mom Abigail says. She goes back to stirring the melted chocolate, and Milla sinks back into the cushions.

" ...is a Cub Scout," Max is saying, "and he wanted me to be one with him, because Thomas doesn't like doing stuff by himself. My mom said it was up to me, but that Boy Scouts don't allow gay people, which she thinks is wrong."

"Wait—are you gay?" Milla asks, confused. Is it even possible for fifth graders to be gay?

"Max is gay?!" Mom Abigail exclaims.

"Mom!" Milla cries. She pulls one of the sofa cushions

119

on top of her and presses the phone to her ear. "Sorry, my mom is being annoying. What?"

"My dad's old roommate from college is gay," Max explains. "He's my godfather, and he comes over for dinner a lot and stuff. But if he wanted to be a Boy Scout, he wouldn't be allowed. The Boy Scouts wouldn't let him in."

"Oh," Milla says, thinking Max's godfather is probably too old to be a Boy Scout now.

"So that's why I decided not to be one." He pauses. "We still buy the popcorn, though. My mom says it gives her a moral crisis every time, but I like it."

"Is it the cheesy kind that comes in a big tub? And the tub has army guys on it?" Both of Katie-Rose's brothers are Boy Scouts, which is how Milla knows about the army guys. The cheesiness reminds her of Yasaman, and she says, "You should check if it has trans fats before you buy any more."

"Okay," Max says. "So . . . do you want to come over tomorrow after school?"

"Hold on," Milla says. She unearths herself from the sofa. "Mom, can I go to Max's house tomorrow?"

"Is he a Girl Scout?" Mom Abigail asks.

Milla thrusts her eyeballs hard at her mom to say, *Omigosh, Mom, will you hush?!*

Mom Abigail's lips twitch. "If you're willing to ride your bike over, sure."

"My mom says yes," Milla tells Max.

"Cool," Max says.

Milla figures it's time to get off the phone, but there's something she's still confused about. "So, do Girl Scouts *not* not allow gay people?"

"Huh?"

"Girl Scouts. Can Girl Scouts be gay?"

"*Oh.* Yes, but they can't be boys." He laughs, and it's such an adorable laugh that Milla can't help but laugh, too. "Plus, they wear skirts."

"You would look good in a green pleated skirt!" Milla says. Then, "Well, no, you wouldn't." They laugh harder.

After they hang up, Milla goes back to her room, where her laptop waits on her bed. When she wakes up the screen, she sees a message from Yasaman in her LuvYaBunches.com inbox. *Sweet!*

She clicks on it. When the screen opens, there's no text. Just a frog. It's staring at her.

"Hi, frog," Milla says.

It keeps staring.

Now why would Yasaman send me a frog and nothing else? Milla wonders.

Not that she minds receiving a frog. She's in such a good mood that Yasaman could send her a picture of a napkin, or a water buffalo, and Milla would be like, *Yay! A water buffalo!*

Then she remembers seeing Yasaman in the media center this morning. She said she was working on something for their website. Speckles? Spoockles?

Milla runs the cursor over the frog, and the frog opens its mouth. She moves the cursor off, and its mouth closes. *Hmm.* She double-clicks on the frog, and a bit of froggy magic happens:

"Hello!" the frog says in a computerized voice. "I hope you is hazzing a good night!"

Milla grins. It's like a LOLcat, but instead it's a LOLfrog! A LOLfrog that *talks*!!!

"I is!" she types back, since she doesn't know how to make talking frogs. "I is hazzing a *very* good nite."

Tuesday, September 20

Thirteen

Yasaman

Tuesday gets off to a bad start. First, word spreads that Modessa won't be coming to school today—and not because she's sick. According to Quin, Modessa isn't coming to school because she doesn't want to apologize to Cyril for poking him on the playground yesterday.

Well, for making *Quin* poke him.

Well, for *encouraging* Quin to poke him. Quin is a big girl and can decide on her own whether to poke someone or not. But Modessa, as Quin's best friend, has a lot of power over Quin, and she uses it in a bad way.

Yasaman doesn't want to be that sort of friend. She thinks it's important to be kind to everyone, even Quin. Unless Quin is a jerk to her, because an exception to the kindness rule is that a person is allowed to stand up for herself. If Quin calls Yasaman "Spazaman," for example, Yasaman can respond with a clever retort. If she thinks of one. Violet is much better at clever retorts than Yasaman, and in situations requiring clever retorts, Yasaman always wishes she could borrow Violet's brain.

When time for morning snack rolls around, the day's not-so-greatness continues. The snack is Cheezy D'lites, and Katie-Rose sighs loudly when Brannen, the snack helper, places a serving on her desk. She clears her throat and looks pointedly at Ms. Perez, who stops in the middle of raising a Cheezy D'lite to her mouth.

"Oh, that's right," she says. "Katie-Rose has something she'd like to say. Katie-Rose?"

To Yasaman's amazement, Katie-Rose stands up, throws back her shoulders, and launches into a lecture about how unhealthy Cheezy D'lites are. How they're made with trans fats, and how trans fats are linked to heart problems, cancer, and obesity. Also how the fake orange color is bad, because it poisons your brain.

At first, Yasaman is surprised, but impressed. She had no idea Katie-Rose was planning this. But the longer Katie-Rose talks, the more theatrical she becomes.

"People in the medical community call trans fats the *silent killer*," Katie-Rose says ominously. She pauses. "That's what *I* call them, too."

Yasaman sinks lower in her seat.

"Do we want to welcome the silent killer into our bodies?" Katie-Rose says. "Do we want to open our mouths and say, 'Come on in, silent killer!'? No! No, we do not! And that is why, on moral and nutritional grounds, I hereby reject the evil known as Cheezy D'lites!"

By now, Yasaman is fully blushing. Yes, she wants to reject the evil known as Cheezy D'lites. But must Katie-Rose be so dramatic?

Apparently, she must. Thrusting her fist into the air, she cries, "All in favor of banning Cheezy D'lites from now till eternity, say *aye*!"

No one says aye. No one says anything. Yasaman

knows she *should* say aye, especially since Katie-Rose is making this grand gesture for her. But couldn't Katie-Rose have passed around a petition instead? Or made an informational brochure and posted it on the Put It Here board in the hall?

Katie-Rose tries again: "All in favor, say *aye!*"

"Aye," Yasaman says in the barest puff of a whisper.

Quin snickers, which breaks the seal for the rest of the kids to snicker, too.

"If you don't want your Cheezy D'lites, just give them to me," Preston says.

"Yeah," Quin says. She's acting surprisingly confident given that her puppet master, Modessa, isn't there. Yasaman is struck by the thought that maybe Quin is a real girl after all. A real fake girl, of course, and obnoxious as all get out, but maybe Quin is actually benefiting from not having Modessa there every minute of the day.

"Cheezy D'lites are awesome," Quin goes on, popping a Cheezy D'lite into her mouth. "They're, like, all-American. Anyone who doesn't like Cheezy D'lites should move to New Zealand."

Color rises in Katie-Rose's cheeks. "I'm sure they have

Cheezy D'lites in New Zealand, too. They might call them something else, but I'm sure they have them."

"See?" Quin retorts.

Katie-Rose turns to Yasaman, and Yasaman feels ill. She hasn't eaten her pile of Cheezy D'lites—and she's not going to—and yet it feels as though she's swallowed a brick of cheese-flavored wrongness.

"All right, everyone, settle down," Ms. Perez says. "Katie-Rose, that was a . . . stirring presentation. You've given us a lot to chew on."

"Like Cheezy D'lites," Preston says, chortling.

Ms. Perez presses her fingers to her forehead, as if she should have seen that coming. To Katie-Rose, or maybe to everyone, she says, "Just remember, everyone is entitled to his or her own opinion."

"And we all agree that Cheezy D'lites rock," Quin says. "Anyway, if you got rid of Cheezy D'lites, what would happen to all the people in the Cheezy D'lites factories? Do you want them to be jobless?"

Katie-Rose frowns, and Yasaman can see she hasn't considered this. Yasaman hasn't, either. "They could make something else."

"Except I'm sure it's not that easy," Quin says. "I'm sure they've got special machines and everything, specifically for making Cheezy D'lites. And if all those workers lost their jobs, what would happen to their children, huh?"

"They'd be homeless," Chance says. He grins. "Homeless and cold, all because you don't like trans fats. Don't you think that's a little selfish, Katie-Rose?"

Katie-Rose is flustered. "No, and it wouldn't be just me making them homeless—*not* that they would be. Yasaman's on my side. Right, Yasaman?"

Yasaman's throat tightens. She nods, but she knows it's not enough. How foolish she was to think she could change the world! She's not brave enough to be a fighter, even for a cause she believes in.

"*I* agree with you, Katie-Rothe," Natalia says from her desk in the front row. She twists to face the class. "Cheethy D'liteth are groth."

Gratitude floods Yasaman's body. She smiles at Natalia, and Natalia smiles back, somewhat primly. She bends down and comes back up with a big ziplock bag, which she plunks onto her desk. It's full of shiny white buttons, the kind you pin to your shirt.

"I think it'th wrong for our very own thchool to make uth eat thomething bad," Natalia says. "Becauth we're kidth, they think we don't matter. But I thay they're wrong. I thay we should thtart a revolution!"

Everyone gets excited, and the mood flips from let's-give-Katie-Rose-a-hard-time to *Weeeeee! Let's go wild!*

"Yeah," Chance says. "We could make signs and march around the school!"

"No," Ms. Perez says, holding her hands out in an attempt to stem the tide.

"We could sneak into the Cheezy D'lites delivery trucks!" Preston says. "We could put ink in the boxes, like that ink they use to stop bank robbers, and when you opened the box, it would dye everyone blue!"

"No, orange, because of the fake cheese," Ava suggests.

"Class? No," Ms. Perez says. "No protest marches, no sneaking into delivery trucks. You all need to calm down."

"Well, I made buttonth if anyone wantth one," Natalia says. She lifts her ziplock bag.

Kids flock to her desk.

"I do. I want one!" Ava says.

"Me too," says Melissa.

Natalia passes them out. Even the boys want one, because everyone loves free stuff.

Chance aims the sharp needle-y part of his at Preston. *"En garde!"* he cries.

"No swords," Ms. Perez says. "Anyone who uses his button as a weapon will lose his button, got it?" She approaches Natalia's desk and fingers the shiny buttons. "These are really cool. Can I have one?"

"Of courth. I made enough for the whole grade." She hands two additional buttons to Ava and says, "Will you pleath give thith to Yathaman? And here'th one for Katie-Rothe."

"No thanks," Katie-Rose says angrily.

But Yasaman accepts hers, and she sees that Ms. Perez is right. Natalia's buttons are cool. Inside a red circle is the word *Trans Fats*, and there's a red slash through it, the universal symbol for saying something's not allowed. Around the outer edge of the circle is the slogan *Why Snackrifice?*

Yasaman peeks at Katie-Rose, who's scowling and slouching in her seat. Yasaman feels a flash of irritation, which she quickly pushes away.

"Okay, gang, time to get back to work," Ms. Perez says. "Put your buttons away and take out your math books, please. Chance? That includes you."

She tells the class what problems to do, and Yasaman gets busy. She keeps thinking about Katie-Rose and the buttons, though. Why is Katie-Rose so mad at Natalia, when Natalia has actually helped their Snack Attack campaign? Isn't Katie-Rose being ... well ... meanish and ungrateful?

A folded-up note lands in her lap. She opens it, expecting it to be from Katie-Rose. Expecting it to maybe say, "Fine, I admit it, the buttons are cool. But Natalia is still annoying. And why didn't you stand up for me when the Snack Attack was your idea in the first place???"

But the note is from Natalia, and instead of calling her out for being such a wimp, it says, *Yay, us!* When Yasaman looks up, she sees Natalia smiling and giving her a thumbs-up. Yasaman smiles awkwardly back.

A few seconds later, and another note lands in her lap. Then another, and another—a whole series of Natalia-notes. One is folded up to be a fortune-teller, and the flaps open to reveal healthy food choices, like tangerines and peanut butter toast. The next says, *So, do you like the buttons?????? You should put yours on!* The one after that says, *I'll give you another if you want. Do you?* And under that, the words YES, NO, and MAYBE, with empty squares next to each.

"Tell her to stop passing you notes!" Katie-Rose whispers from the desk beside her.

Yasaman tries to ignore her, because there's no talking during math. She wishes Natalia would stop passing her notes, too, because there's not supposed to be note-passing, either.

Katie-Rose kicks the leg of Yasaman's desk.

"Let me read them," she whispers. "Let me read them, and *I'll* write back!"

At the front of the room, Natalia waves furtively to get Yasaman's attention. "Pick one!" she mouths, using hand gestures to mime putting a check mark in one of the squares.

Yasaman has never had two people fighting over her. Some girls would probably like it, being pegged with notes and jostled by kicks, even if the kicks had anger in them. They would be like, *Ha ha ha, and whom should I bestow my favor upon today? Ha ha ha, of course, everyone wants to be my friend!*

But Yasaman hates it. She glues her eyes to her math book and grips her pencil.

Katie-Rose kicks her desk again.

Natalia bends down, trying to worm her way into Yasaman's vision.

"Girls?" Ms. Perez says. She looks in turn at Katie-Rose, Natalia, *and* Yasaman. "Is there a problem?"

"No, ma'am," Yasaman whispers.

"No, ma'am," Natalia jumps in. "Thorry."

"Katie-Rose?"

Katie-Rose has pale skin, so when she blushes, it's extremely noticeable. Right now she's the color of a ripe tomato.

"No, ma'am," Katie-Rose mutters.

"Mmm," Ms. Perez says, meaning, *Then let's do our work, shall we?*

Yasaman returns to her math problem, trying to focus on train number one, which is heading west at fifty miles an hour, and train number two, which is heading east even faster. Presumably, they won't ram into each other, because things in fifth-grade math books tend not to explode.

Yasaman prays the same is true for her classroom.

fourteen

Camilla

What a great day it is! SUCH a great day. Milla is floaty with happiness, and if not for the laws of nature, she'd surely rise up from her desk like a girl-shaped balloon. She'd bob around above everyone, smiling down, and as she got the hang of being weightless, she'd do tricks, even. Like a flip!

She glances at Max, who is the reason for her floatiness. Why? Well, because he's *Max*, and he's smart and sweet and adorable. Also because of what happened at the pencil sharpener five minutes ago. They both got up to sharpen their pencils at the exact same time—

coincidence? or fate?!—and he said, "Do you want to hear a joke?"

It was about a duck who went to a bar, but instead of ordering a drink, he asked the bartender if he had any grapes.

"No," the bartender said. "This is a bar. Why would I have grapes?"

So the duck waddled out of the bar, and then waddled right back in two seconds later. "Hi there!" he said. "You got any grapes?"

"*No,*" the bartender said. "I don't have any grapes. Sheesh!"

This happened again and again, until finally the bartender said, "Listen, duck. If you ask me for grapes one more time, I will flip you upside down and nail you to the wall by your feet!" Which Milla and Max agreed was a terrible thing for that bartender to say, because *ouch!* Or to use Max's phrase, *owwie ow ow,* and when Milla said that, Max grinned.

"So the duck waddled out of the bar," Max said, "but, two seconds later, in he waddled again."

"Uh-oh," Milla said.

"But this time he said to the bartender, 'Hi there! You got any nails?' And the bartender got really mad and said, 'No!!!'"

Max held Milla's gaze. Milla's lips twitched, ready to smile.

"So the duck said, 'Well, then, you got any grapes?'"

Milla laughed, and Max looked happy, and his happiness fed into hers. The knowledge that she'd be going to his house this afternoon made her even happier, and happiness bounced back and forth between them like a super ball.

Now Max is back in his seat, and it takes him a minute to feel Milla's glance. But then he does, and when their eyes meet—*whoosh!* Milla's chest expands.

"Attention up here, guys," Mr. Emerson says, snapping his fingers. "There's something we need to talk about, and it's not pretty. But it's out there, and it's not going away." He pauses. "The elephant in the room, my friends? *Puberty.*"

Heat travels up Milla's body. Why do words like *puberty,* which are totally embarrassing in terms of what they mean, also have to *sound* so embarrassing? Take the word *lamp*. There is nothing embarrassing about *lamp,* or *table*, or *pork loin.*

No, that's not true. *Pork loin* is semi-embarrassing, but not nearly as bad as *puberty.* Mr. Emerson is always tossing random and possibly inappropriate comments into their class discussions, and usually Milla loves it. Like just last week, he shared with his students an *aha* moment he'd had regarding nose hair. "Yes, gang," he said, "you can buy actual nose hair trimmers made specifically for that purpose. After careful consideration, I went with the Turbo-Groomer Five Point O." He tilted his head, nostrils to the ceiling. "I think we can all agree that it lives up to its name, yes?"

But it's one thing to discuss embarrassing details about himself, and another to bring up embarrassing topics that are specific to fifth graders. Must he really discuss puberty when he's supposed to be making them do their vocabulary?

"I'm talking about sweat," he says. "Body odor. I don't say this to make anyone uncomfortable, but I've noticed that our room sometimes has a funky smell, and I know it's not me."

Everyone titters, or almost everyone. Cyril Remkiwicz doesn't. He's scrawling away in his notebook, the notebook that has nothing to do with schoolwork.

There is something about Cyril that Milla feels bad about: He does, on occasion, smell, and she wonders if Mr. Emerson is maybe thinking of him as he talks to the class about deodorant and daily showers. He's not even listening, though. Is he?

She peers at him from under a swoop of hair. He does look slightly uncomfortable, so maybe he's just pretending not to listen. Or maybe he isn't feeling well. He puts down his pen, closes his eyes, and presses his hand against his stomach.

"And use shampoo," Mr. Emerson continues. "You kids are at the age when you're going to need to wash your hair more frequently, every other day or even every day."

Milla nods. She's all for clean, shiny hair. Max's hair is thick and kind of crazy in the way it sticks up all over the place, but it's always clean, so she knows Mr. Emerson isn't talking to him. Anyway, Max *might* even wear cologne. Milla can't swear to it, but standing beside him at the pencil sharpener, she caught a whiff of pine trees and toothpaste. Colgate, the Great Regular Flavor.

"All right, then," he says. "Are we good? Are you guys going to keep your faces clean and your armpits deodorized?"

The class laughs, even Milla—even though she doesn't yet wear deodorant. Should she? *Omigosh,* how horrible it would be if she had body odor like Cyril, and she didn't even know it! She's 99 percent sure she doesn't. But what if she did???

"Terrific," Mr. Emerson says. "I'm glad we had this talk, as I, for one, feel closer to each and every one of you. I'm sure you feel the same. And now, take out your vocab and turn to this week's lesson."

There is a widespread opening of desks. As Milla fishes out her workbook, her eyes dart to Max. She doesn't consciously decide to peek at him. It just happens.

Max's eyes meet hers—*omigosh,* he's looking at her, too!—and she smiles foolishly. Just as foolishly, he smiles back.

Fifteen

Katie-Rose

There's a picture book Katie-Rose's mom used to read to her called *When Sophie Gets Angry, Really Really Angry*. Her mom read it to her *a lot,* and it took Katie-Rose longer than it should have to realize why: Her mom was secretly thinking about all the times Katie-Rose got angry, really really angry, and hoping the boo would give her coping strategies and stuff.

Once Katie-Rose figured this out, she accidentally-o purpose returned *When Sophie Gets Angry* to the publ library, when it had never been a library book in the fir place. Katie-Rose didn't have anger management issues, not then and not now. *Please.*

But as Natalia passes what has to be her fifty-millionth note to Yasaman, Katie-Rose finds herself wondering if maybe she does. She wants to punch Natalia in the face, which she suspects is not the reaction of a calm and levelheaded person.

Or maybe Natalia is just amazingly irritating. Maybe—no, not maybe, *definitely*—Natalia has friend-stealing issues, and Katie-Rose's urge to punch her is completely justified.

She digs her fingernails into her palms as Yasaman reads this most recent note. (Although, why *is* Yasaman reading the note? Why has Yasaman read any of the notes? Doesn't she know she's just encouraging Natalia?)

Stop it, she tells herself, not wanting to think bad houghts about her friend. It's much better to think bad oughts about Natalia, and plus there are so many to oose from.

Like how in third grade, Natalia stood so close to her PE that Katie-Rose didn't have enough room to do e hula hoop, which made everyone assume she was physically incapable of doing the hula hoop, which was utterly ridiculous as Katie-Rose could do the hula hoop for thirty minutes straight in her own driveway. Yes, she timed herself, and yes, if it wasn't for Natalia sucking her hula-hoop love right out of her, she probably would have been a national champion by now.

Then, in fourth grade, Natalia beat Katie-Rose in the geography bee. It was a travesty. Katie-Rose sat in a row of chairs with the other nine finalists while the rest of the school looked on. Each kid got asked a question from a special booklet the principal had. Ms. Westerfeld wasn't allowed to choose which question to ask. She had to follow specific rules and all that.

The group of finalists went from ten to five, and then from five to two, and the two were Katie-Rose and Natalia.

Natalia's final-round question was, "What is the capital of California?" Which was so easy, because they lived in California! So of course Natalia got it right!

Then it was Katie-Rose's turn. If she answered her question correctly, they'd have a tiebreaker round. If not, Natalia would be the winner.

Ms. Westerfeld ran her finger down the page of the

booklet. Her eyebrows went up, and Katie-Rose's muscles clenched. Then—far worse—Ms. Westerfeld smoothed out her concern and blandly read out Katie-Rose's question.

"What South Carolina coastal area is home to one of the largest populations of loggerhead turtles in the country?" she asked.

Well, who in the world knew *that,* except maybe a kid from South Carolina? *Now* Katie-Rose knows, because it was burned into her memory. It's some beachy place called DeBordieu. Big-flapping-fantastic.

But back then, at the critical moment, Katie-Rose got it wrong, and she knew in her heart Natalia would have, too. And yet Natalia was declared the champion, and she received a special certificate with a special seal. A month later, she got to miss school to attend the citywide competition, but she didn't win that time, so *ha ha.*

Katie-Rose knows she's not being very mature. She even knows that in the BIG PICTURE, the stupid fourth-grade geography bee was just that: a stupid fourth-grade geography bee. Who cares who won, especially now, a whole year later?

But there is the problem with that argument: In the BIG PICTURE, Natalia hasn't gotten better with time. First she stole Katie-Rose's hula hoop Olympic gold medal, then she stole Katie-Rose's geography bee victory, *and now she's trying to steal Katie-Rose's BFF.*

She *is,* only Yasaman can't see it since Natalia's being as nice as pie to Yasaman.

A crease forms in Katie-Rose's forehead as Natalia folds a new note into a triangle, like those paper footballs the boys make and shoot across their desks. She cups the note in her hand and reaches her arms behind her, pretending to stretch. Katie-Rose perches on the end of her chair.

Ms. Perez calls on Olivia to do the next math problem, and Natalia listens attentively, the perfect student. Behind her back, she flips her wrist, and the note arcs through the air and lands with a soft *plimp* by Yasaman's desk.

Katie-Rose doesn't think. She just acts. She lunges, snatches, and is back in her seat before Yasaman can blink. With fumbling fingers, she unfolds the piece of paper and reads Natalia's message:

Oh, and one more thing. It's true what I said about Coke and Pepsi. I've never tasted either one, not even a sip. I just wanted to say that because some people—NOT you—didn't seem to believe me.

Katie-Rose crumples the note, because, *grrrrrrr!* Natalia is such a liar! Again, and Katie-Rose will say it till the day she dies, there is no way anyone in America can live to be ten years old without trying at least a sip of pop. Most ten-year-olds have drunk a gazillion-squillion gallons of the stuff, if not more. Katie-Rose certainly has.

Some might say—like Katie-Rose's mom, for instance—"Oh, Katie-Rose, who cares? You'll only make things worse by getting all dramatic about it." Katie-Rose can't live that way, though. Undramatically. Not when someone is lying in order to make Katie-Rose look bad. Not when that same someone is trying to wedge a crowbar between Katie-Rose and her BFF, hoping to kick Katie-Rose out and slide into her spot!

The thought of Natalia taking her place in Yasaman's heart makes Katie-Rose feel as if she were standing at the edge of a dark and bottomless pit. Katie-Rose has worried in the past about losing Milla to some unspeakable evil (like Modessa and Quin), and as for Violet, Katie-Rose still marvels that such a cool and collected girl would choose to be her friend. But the possibility of Yasaman replacing her with someone else . . .

She can't think about that. She *can't*. She fantasizes, instead, about exposing Natalia's lies so that Yasaman will know what a fake she is. Maybe she'll buy one of those teddy bears with a video camera hidden inside and plant it in Natalia's room so she can catch Natalia's fakeness on film. Or no, she should put it in Natalia's kitchen, since that's where the refrigerator is. No doubt filled with Coke *and* Pepsi!

Maybe the video camera should be disguised as a vase of flowers instead of a teddy bear, and the center of one of the flowers could be the camera lens. *Ha ha,* that would be perfect, a flower capturing Natalia's soft-drink-chugging downfall!

"Watch," Katie-Rose would say to Yasaman after uploading the incriminating video to LuvYaBunches.com.

"I don't understand," Yasaman would say.

"You will soon," Katie-Rose would reply. Then she'd hit the Play button on her laptop.

FADE IN TO KATIE-ROSE'S FANTASY SEQUENCE:

INTERIOR NATALIA'S HOUSE—KITCHEN—
LATE AFTERNOON

Natalia skips into the kitchen and drops her backpack
on the table.

NATALIA
(to no one)
I'm ho-ome! And boy, am I parched. All that lying
thure doeth make a girl thirthty!

She notices a vase of roses on the granite island.

NATALIA (CONT'D)
Ooo, flowerth. Pretty!

She leans in to smell them, and her massive headgear
gleams. Then her nose wrinkles, and her upper lip
twitches. Her eyelids flutter uncontrollably.

NATALIA (CONT'D)

Ah . . . ah . . . ah-choo!

She wipes a snot worm from her nose with the back of her hand, and then she wipes her hand on her jeans. It leaves a smear. It is disgusting. But Natalia doesn't care. She skips to the refrigerator and takes out a two-liter bottle of Coca-Cola.

NATALIA (CONT'D)

Mmm, Coke! I love Coke! And Pepthi, too. Mmm!

She uncaps the bottle, tilts it to her mouth, and chugs. She downs the entire bottle—and then, quite unexpectedly, she gets a weird look on her face. She approaches the vase of roses and leans in.

NATALIA (CONT'D)

(staring straight into the camera lens)

Who'th thpying on me?

The image wavers.

Ith that you, Katie-Rothe? Ooo, you are in tho
much trouble!

DISSOLVE TO:

"—don't want to ask again," Ms. Perez says, exasperated. "I expect more from you than this, Katie-Rose."

From the front row, Natalia makes a sound that's
almost, but not quite, a snicker. Yasaman, who's now
sitting next to Natalia—(wait a second, how did that
happen?)—shakes her head at Natalia, like *Don't*. The
fact that Yasaman sticks up for Katie-Rose makes Katie-
Rose feel better, but only for a second. What is Yasaman
doing in the front row with Natalia?

Katie-Rose looks at Yasaman's desk, which is now
occupied by Chance. She's completely confused.

"Katie-Rose," Ms. Perez says. "Take your workbook
and join Ava *now*."

Obviously, Katie-Rose has missed a big chunk of Ms.
Perez's instructions. She grabs her workbook and goes to
Ava, feeling dumb and out of sorts.

"We're doing the next problem set with partners," Ava whispers.

"We are?" Katie-Rose says. She doesn't sit down, because there's no chair for her. "When did that happen?"

"Um, just now?"

"Did Ms. Perez assign us partners, or did she let us pick?"

Ava regards Katie-Rose uneasily. "She let us pick. You didn't have a partner, so . . ." She lifts her shoulders.

Katie-Rose's breaths grow shallow. If they picked their own partners, why is Yasaman in the front of the room with Natalia? Why isn't she back here, with her?

Unless Natalia claimed her and *made* her be her partner while Katie-Rose was off in la-la land. *Omigosh*, that has to be what happened. The nerve of that girl!!!

Katie-Rose marches to Natalia's desk.

"Yasaman is *my* partner," she declares. "You leave her alone, Natalia. And Yasaman, *you* need to just—" Just what? And is she really saying this, in front of the whole class?

She needs to pull it together. She *can't* pull it together, and Natalia is gaping at her, her pale face like a trapped moon inside the cage of her headgear.

"You need to stop talking to Natalia, period!" she says. "I officially forbid you from talking to her anymore!"

Natalia bursts into fake tears, only her sobs are so loud—so *wild*—that Katie-Rose's heart speeds up.

"Come on, Yasaman," she says shrilly. "Let's go."

Yasaman stays seated, staring at the crazy lunatic wearing the Katie-Rose suit. That's what it feels like. *Everyone* stares at the crazy lunatic wearing the Katie-Rose suit, and the real Katie-Rose, the one who isn't a shrill bossy-boss, wishes desperately she could rip the wretched thing off and go back to being normal.

Katie-Rose steps back. She bumps into Ms. Perez, who has come up behind her.

"Out," Ms. Perez says, pointing at the door.

"Wh-what?"

Ms. Perez, normally so bubbly and warm, looks at Katie-Rose as if she doesn't even *like* her anymore. "You can do your work in the hall."

Katie-Rose gulps and turns to Natalia, whose sobs have tapered off.

"I'm sorry, Natalia. I'm really, really sorry."

Natalia starts up again, wailing as if her kitten has just died. Katie-Rose waves her arms helplessly.

"What I did was a bad decision," she tells Ms. Perez. "I know that now, and I'm sorry, and I promise I'll be quiet and not disrupt the class anymore. Okay?"

"Go sit in the hall, Katie-Rose," Ms. Perez says.

Katie-Rose looks at Yasaman, who drops her gaze. This is the worst blow of all. She feels dizzy, and though she's never fainted before, she thinks this might be a good time to start. Then everybody would feel bad for *her*, and fuss over *her*, and Natalia's sobbing would be forgotten. Ms. Perez would like her again, and so would Yasaman.

She walks toward the door on legs that are strangely light. Chance cowers as she passes, making a show of holding up his hands to protect himself.

"Was it the Cheezy D'lites?" Chance says in a stage whisper. "Did they poison your brain?"

No one laughs until she's out of the room.

And then, they do.

Sixteen

After lunch—at which Katie-Rose was conspicuously absent, and Yasaman was vague about why—Violet gets called to the office. When she arrives, she sees Cyril Remkiwicz over by the copying machine, and her first thought is that she's been called in to talk about the poking game on the playground. But Cyril is lying on a blue mat like the ones the preschoolers use at naptime, which tells Violet he must be sick. Rivendell doesn't have an infirmary, or a school nurse, so the blue mat is where kids rest while they're waiting to be picked up by a parent. Maybe her being called to the office has nothing to do with Cyril after all.

Either way, Violet feels bad for Cyril, but not so bad that she's tempted to go give him a hug or anything. *Euggh,* she thinks. Then she feels not-nice. But then she reminds herself that thinking *euggh* about someone is different than poking someone for points and then refusing to apologize, and, in Modessa's case, skipping school to get out of it.

Also, sometimes bad thoughts come into your mind whether you invite them or not. In fact, the more you try not to think something, the stronger that thought becomes. Violet saw that happen to her mom in those last awful weeks before she went to the hospital, when her hand shook so much she couldn't apply her lipstick. She would gaze at herself in the mirror, with Violet standing behind her shoulder, and she'd say, "Oh, Violet, I'm such a bad mother. *Such* a bad mother. Such a bad mother!"

"Mom," Violet would say. She felt so helpless. She'd take the lipstick from the vanity and stand in front of her mother, blocking her reflection. "Hold still. You look beautiful, Mom."

Hovering outside the main office, Violet closes her eyes. Her therapist, back in Atlanta, told her, "Don't push too hard, Violet. When an unwanted thought comes, acknowledge it and move on. Don't fight it, or it will fight back."

She opens her eyes to find Cyril Remkiwicz staring at her, his head turned on the blue mat. His shirt today has a zebra on it with the head of a fish. It's as if he *wants* to be unnatural, or point to the unnatural, or suggest that the whole world is unnatural.

She goes to the secretary, a skinny man straight out of college named Mr. McGreevy. Mr. McGreevy is from England and has an accent that makes everything he says sound charming.

"Hi," Violet says. "I got a note to come see you?"

Mr. McGreevy holds up a finger. "One sec, love." He straightens up from his filing, pushes his shock of hair off his forehead, and smiles. "Ah, Violet. Yes. Your mum phoned, wants you to phone her back."

Violet goes stock-still.

"Nothing bad, love," McGreevy goes on, concerned by Violet's response. "Just wants a quick chat?"

But... mothers aren't supposed to call their daughters at school for "a quick chat." Is it because she rarely takes her mom's calls at home, ducking the obligation by holing up in her room, or by conveniently choosing to take a shower during the slot of time inpatients are allowed to use the community phone?

Violet has allowed two full weeks to go by without talking to her mother, and now it's coming back to bite her. Her eyes slide to Cyril, but she drags them back. If he's listening, she doesn't want to know.

Mr. McGreevy lifts the phone from its base and hands it to Violet, who takes it robotically. It's an old-fashioned office phone with a cord. Violet is tethered to the front desk.

"I'll punch in the number for you?" Mr. McGreevy says. He shuffles through the post-its on his desk. "Ah, yes. You'll be routed through the nurse's station—I s'pose you know the drill—and they'll patch you through."

Violet feels like she's stepped through the looking glass. Mr. McGreevy knows her mom is in the hospital?

Does he know which one, and which ward? Do all the staff members at Rivendell know? Do the students?!

Violet puts her hand on the desk to steady herself.

The phone is ringing. Violet hears the faraway sound of it even though she has yet to bring it to her ear. Mr. McGreevy arches his eyebrows, and Violet lifts the receiver.

"California State Regional Hospital," a lady blares. Violet presses the phone tight-tight-tight to her ear, hoping to keep the lady's shrill voice from escaping the black plastic.

"I was hoping . . . you could, um, connect me . . ." Violet folds in on herself, hating how exposed she feels.

"Patient's name?" the lady asks.

"Lavinia Truitt," Violet whispers.

"I can't hear you. Could you please speak up?"

"Lavinia Truitt," Violet says, hating herself, hating Mr. McGreevy, hating Cyril, who *better* not be listening.

"Lavinia Truitt," the lady repeats. There is a pause, and Violet imagines the lady running her finger down a list, or scrolling through a computerized directory. "There we go. The locked ward uses a different code, but I've found her."

What, was she lost? Violet thinks. She doesn't want an answer to that question, actually. Mothers shouldn't be in locked wards. People shouldn't say the words *locked ward.*

"I'm connecting you now," the lady says.

"Wait!" Violet says, suddenly panicked.

Too late. There is dead air, and then a spot of horrible elevator music, and then a click. Her mother's voice, breathless. "Violet?"

"Mom," Violet says. Her skin flushes. The ache inside her threatens to swallow her whole.

"Violet. Baby. I miss you so much, Boo. You know that, right?"

A lump forms in Violet's throat. *I miss you, too,* her heart says.

"I talked to Daddy," her mother says. "He says you've made some good friends?"

Daddy. Violet hasn't called her dad "Daddy" since they moved here from Atlanta. And her mom is no longer *Mommy,* and Violet is no longer a little girl.

"I need to see you, Boo," her mom says softly.

Well, tough! Violet thinks with a flare of anger.

You should have thought about that before getting so depressed! It's so true about how bad thoughts enter your brain whether you invite them in or not.

"I miss you, Violet," her mom says.

Violet lowers her voice. "I miss you, too, Mom."

"Will you come soon? Will you come today?"

"I can't. Dad's working late. How would I get to the hospital?"

She detects movement from her peripheral vision. Cyril has lifted his head; he seems to be listening in on her conversation. *Oh crap,* she thinks. What, exactly, did she just say? Did she say "hospital"? She did, didn't she? *Oh crap.*

"Tomorrow?" her mom says.

"Fine," Violet says. Her voice is ragged, and Mr. McGreevy glances up from his paperwork.

"You will?" her mom presses. "You won't forget, or change your mind?"

"Yes, Mom. I mean, *no.* I mean, I've got to go."

"Yes, you'll come, or no, you won't?"

Shut up! Violet thinks. *And stop staring at me! If everybody would just shut up and stop staring at me!*

"Yes, I'll come," she says tersely. "I've got to go now."

"But—"

"Bye, Mom." She hangs up, catching a scattering of her mom's final flutter of words. *Understand. Love. Tomorrow.*

Cyril is still looking at her, his eyes flat and black.

Seventeen

Camilla

illa folds her hand into a fist in front of Max's door, because that's what you do when you show up at somebody's house. (After going home and changing outfits and brushing your hair and stuff. And popping a peppermint Lifesaver into your mouth for freshness.) Anyway, once you get to someone's house, you knock. And maybe it's scary if you're, like, selling something, because who knows? The person who answers could growl, "Hi, little Girl Scout. NO, I DON'T WAN̶̶̶ COOKIES!"

She giggles. *There is no reason to be scared,* she coaches herself. *Knock.*

Her hand hovers.

Knock on the door!!!

Right as she goes for it, the door opens, and Milla's momentum throws her forward into Max.

"Oh!" she cries. He smells like toothpaste. He looks embarrassed as he steadies Milla and pushes her back into a normal position. Well, Milla is embarrassed, too. She giggles.

"Hi," she says. When he doesn't respond, she adds, "I'm here to meet Stewy."

"I know," Max says. "But, uh . . ."

His ears are red, Milla notices. And his mom is standing behind him in the entry hall. A set of car keys connected to a silver loop dangles from her index finger.

"We need to get going, Max," she says. She smiles at Milla apologetically. "Hi. You're Milla?"

Milla nods, confused.

"Sorry for the misunderstanding," Max's mom says kindly. "I hope you'll come back another time?"

Milla turns to Max. He's bright red. Not just his ears, but his whole face.

"I have tap today," he confesses.

"Tap?" she says, confused. She takes in his outfit: fluffy gray shorts, a loose-fitting T-shirt, and white socks, pulled all the way up. Dangling from his hand, a pair of shiny black tap shoes. "*Oh.* I didn't know you took tap dancing."

"I didn't, either," Max says. "I mean, I forgot."

It's sinking in that Milla won't be meeting Stewy today, little tuxedo or no little tuxedo. She put on cute shorts and biked all the way over here. She screwed up her courage to knock on the door. And now? Nothing.

She's supposed to leave, she guesses, so she turns on her heel. She hears Max speak urgently to his mom, but she can't hear what he's saying over the rush in her head. She's reached her bike by the time he catches up with her.

"Milla," he says. He's out of breath.

She tries not to let her face show anything, but there is a wideness to her eyes that she can't help.

"You could come tomorrow morning," Max suggests.

"And then my mom could take you to school, if you want. Do you want to?"

Tomorrow *morning*? That's strange, a morning playdate. Not that it's a *playdate*, or any kind of date! But it's also sweet. It means he wants to reschedule ASAP. A smile creeps across Milla's face. "Okay. I'll see if my mom can drop me off on her way to work."

"Max, baby, we've got to go," Max's mom calls.

Max takes off, but Milla's smile stays right where it is. This is the second time Max has asked her to do something, and so what if it's the same something as the first time? It *is* like being asked out on a date, she decides. Kind of.

She imagines the message she'll send Yasaman when she gets home. It will include frog smiley—no, a hamster—and underneath, the words *Omigosh!! I haz date!!!*

Eighteen

Katie-Rose

Katie-Rose can't stop thinking about Natalia. She lies on her bed, rigid as a corpse, trying to build an airtight case against her that proves how Natalia is made of wrong and Katie-Rose is made of right.

It would be easier if Natalia had yelled at Katie-Rose in class and made her cry, instead of the other way around.

And if Katie-Rose hadn't issued that ridiculous command about how Yasaman could no longer talk to Natalia—not one word, ever—that would have been good, too. It would have been helpful in terms of making Natalia out to be the bad guy instead of Katie-Rose.

Natalia *is* the bad guy. Unfortunately, Katie-Rose sees how she might have left room for misinterpretation on that point.

"Here's the thing," Katie-Rose tells the dimpled eggshell-colored plaster of her ceiling. She scowls. What *is* the thing? *Something* is the thing, that's for sure. And it's *not her*. The yuckiness Katie-Rose is feeling is not her fault. So whose fault is it?

"Katie-Rose?" her babysitter, Chrissy, calls. She raps lightly on her bedroom door. "Sure you don't want to watch TV with me? *Modern Family* is on."

"No, thanks," Katie-Rose says. She likes Chrissy. She likes her a lot. But Chrissy is sunny and bright, and Katie-Rose is a sad and grumpy rain cloud. "I prefer to be alone."

"Okay," Chrissy says dubiously. "If you change your mind, I've got ice cream."

Katie-Rose hears her clomp back downstairs, and despair presses Katie-Rose's spine into her mattress. The rest of Katie-Rose's family is off doing boring things: Her brothers are at karate, and her parents are having a "coffee date," and the truth is, she *doesn't* prefer to be alone. Being alone, as it turns out, is lonely.

She sits up, swings her legs off her bed, and goes downstairs. She plunks down on the arm of the sofa where Chrissy is sitting, grabs the remote, and hits the Mute button.

"A*hem*," she says.

Chrissy looks at her, ice-cream spoon paused midway to her mouth. "Yes?"

Katie-Rose slides onto the actual sofa cushion, right up next to Chrissy. It's a tight fit. Katie-Rose has to use her hip to wedge herself in.

"I need your advice," she says.

"Excellent, as I am a fabulous advice giver," Chrissy says. "Spill."

Katie-Rose fills Chrissy in on the Yasaman-and-Natalia situation, and Chrissy listens. Katie-Rose's rant is long enough that Chrissy is able to finish her ice cream, and when Katie-Rose finally reaches the end, Chrissy leans forward and plunks her bowl on the coffee table.

"Hmm," she says. "This is complicated."

"I know."

"I thought Milla was the girl you were having friend problems with."

"That was like a month ago."

"Well, what does *she* have to say about this?"

"Milla?"

"Yes, Milla. Does she have an opinion?"

"No," Katie-Rose says quickly.

"Have you asked?"

"Not exactly."

"What about Yasaman?" Chrissy asks. "Have you told her how Natalia specifically told you she was planning to steal Yasaman away?"

Katie-Rose squirms, reluctant to explain that she might not have quoted Natalia in a way that would hold up in court. It *was* the gist of what Natalia said, though.

"If you haven't, you should," Chrissy says. "And I still don't understand the 'partner' thing. Did Yasaman choose Natalia, or did Natalia choose Yasaman? And you were doing *what* all that time, while people's partners were being picked?"

"Enough questions!" Katie-Rose says. "I thought you were going to give me answers, not ask five thousand zillion questions!"

"Hmm," Chrissy says. She touches the fingers of her

right hand to the fingers of her left hand. "So as I see it, the bottom line is that you're worried Yasaman doesn't like you anymore. Am I right?"

"No!"

"But you said—"

"No, I said it *seems* like Yasaman doesn't like me anymore. *Seems.*"

Chrissy nods, but the way she does so gives Katie-Rose a bad feeling.

"What?" Katie-Rose demands. "You're thinking something."

"Well, yes. I'm thinking that whether Yasaman likes you or not isn't the issue. The issue is, do *you* like you?"

Katie-Rose's jaw drops open. Then she snaps it shut. Her face heats up.

"Do you, Katie-Rose? Do you like yourself?"

Katie-Rose hates Chrissy a little. "Forget it," she says, standing.

"No, wait," Chrissy says. She pulls Katie-Rose back down. "That came out wrong."

You think? Katie-Rose would say if she trusted her voice.

"Anyway, who am I to talk? *I* do stupid things. I do stupid things all the time."

Katie-Rose eyes her. "Like what?"

Chrissy lets her head fall back on the sofa. "Oh my God, so many things. Like, last week I got jealous of this guy for absolutely no good reason. His name's Jellico. Well, that's what we call him."

Katie-Rose nods. Chrissy has talked about Jellico before, about how lots of girls in Chrissy's grade like him, including Chrissy's friend, Hulya. Hulya is Yasaman's cousin, which makes their tenth-grade drama all the more interesting.

"Jellico's in my math class, and last Friday . . ." She swivels her head so that she's looking at Katie-Rose. "You can't tell. This is between us."

"Okay."

"He told me he likes Hulya."

"He did?" Katie-Rose doesn't want to get it wrong, so she chooses her words carefully. "But that's good, right? That out of all the girls who like him, he picked her?"

Chrissy arches one eyebrow, like *is it?* Then she exhales. "Yes. Yes, it is. It's awesome, only I messed up. I *told* you I do stupid things."

"What did you do?"

"Something."

"What?!"

Chrissy gazes at Katie-Rose, and Katie-Rose holds her gaze, even though it makes her heart pound.

"I didn't want Hulya ... to go away," Chrissy says.

Katie-Rose doesn't understand.

"I was jealous. I was *wrong*. But I guess I was afraid that if Hulya and Jellico started going out . . ." Her shoulders go up. "Where would that leave me?"

Katie-Rose knits her brows. "So when Jellico told you he liked Hulya ..."

"I told Hulya he liked this other girl named Chelsea."

"But—"

"I know."

"Jellico *himself* said—"

Chrissy holds her palms out like a cop. "I know!"

Katie-Rose decides it's kindest to move on from this topic, even though she finds it fascinating.

"Jellico is a weird name," she says. "And you're not stupid. Boys are."

"You got that right, sister."

"Fifth-grade boys especially," Katie-Rose says, remembering how Chance cowered when she walked past him, after Ms. Perez banished her from class. Later, on the playground, Chance spotted Katie-Rose and fled from her with floppy, upraised arms, screaming, *"Ahhhhhhh! Attack of the poisoned Cheezy D'lites!"*

Chrissy clasps Katie-Rose's hands. "Listen. I may not have helped with your friend situation, but annoying boys are my specialty. In fact, I've developed several patented techniques for dealing with annoying people in general, girls *and* boys. Shall I give you some pointers, little rabbit?"

Katie-Rose considers. Chrissy has no trouble doing things that make her look weird, which is why her brothers consider her to be a superpretty Froot Loop. Chrissy's "pointers," if acted on, might very well make Katie-Rose look Froot Loopy-ish, too.

But Katie-Rose admires Froot Loop–iness in a girl.

"Yes, please," Katie-Rose tells Chrissy. "I need all the pointers I can get."

Wednesday, September 21

Nineteen

Yasaman

Yasaman and Nigar are ready for school before their *ana* is, because it takes their mother forever to put on her lipstick and line her eyes with kohl eyeliner. She likes to look fancy when she takes Nigar to preschool. Fifth graders can be dropped off outside the building, but preschoolers have to be walked in by a grown-up. Recently, Nigar's drop-offs have been kind of rough.

Today Nigar has on a pink sweatsuit and pink shoes with Velcro straps she can do and undo herself, while Yasaman is wearing black skinny jeans (Yasaman's first pair ever!), a long-sleeved shirt with horizontal black-and-white stripes, and a patterned black *hijab* layered over a soft white underscarf. For shoes, black-and-white checkered Vans, still clean and new looking.

Everything she has on is a hand-me-down from her cousin Hulya, and Yasaman feels lucky to have such a stylish cousin. Hulya's discarded clothes are cuter than anything in Yasaman's own closet, while still being "entirely appropriate for a young Muslim girl," according to her aunt Teyze.

Yet despite the thrill of new old-clothes, Yasaman is troubled. She can't stop thinking about Katie-Rose and Natalia.

Yasaman is used to Katie-Rose going too far with things, but the way Katie-Rose has been treating Natalia goes *beyond* too far. Is Katie-Rose just jealous? Or is she mad at Yasaman, and for some reason taking it out on Natalia?

Yasaman called Katie-Rose last night, but Katie-Rose's babysitter answered and said Katie-Rose wasn't there. But why would Katie-Rose's parents hire a babysitter for a not-there Katie-Rose???

Maybe Yasaman should call Milla and talk to her about it—except, no, because today is the day Milla is going over early to Max's house. Milla told Yasaman about the change of plans yesterday, and also how Max takes tap-dancing lessons, which made both girls giggle.

Milla is probably at Max's already, or at least on the way. Yasaman could call Violet, though. She picks up the kitchen phone and punches in Violet's number. *She might be there, or she might not,* Yasaman tells herself, preparing herself for disappointment.

"Hello?" Violet says.

"Violet!" Yasaman says. "Hi!"

"What's up, girlfriend?" Violet says. Yasaman starts to reply, but Violet rides over her with, "Ooo, hold on. Gotta get my waffle out of the toaster oven. It's chocolate chip, and I hate it when the chips get too melty."

In the background, Yasaman hears moving-around sounds and Violet saying, "Ow, hot." Yasaman isn't allowed to have frozen chocolate chip waffles, partly because they're not good for you and partly because a traditional Turkish breakfast doesn't involve sugar and pastries. Yasaman's own breakfast this morning consisted of olives, tomatoes, and *tam yağli,* the rich, salty cheese her *baba* loves.

Finally, Violet is back. "Sorry 'bout that. You were saying?"

Yasaman's throat tightens. She finds that she doesn't know how to explain what she's feeling, so she dives in with the facts instead. "I called Katie-Rose last night. But her babysitter said she wasn't there."

"Really?" Violet says. "Katie-Rose and I IMed at around eight, so she was there then."

"Oh," Yasaman says. She tries to block the image of Katie-Rose whispering *no, no, no* to her babysitter and backing away from the phone. "Um, what did you IM about?"

"Random stuff, mainly. Although ..."

"What?"

"She *was* kind of mad at you."

Yasaman's spine tingles. "She was? About what?"

"She told some long story about how you were partners with Natalia instead of her. I got kinda lost, to tell the truth."

"But I didn't *want* to be Natalia's partner," Yasaman

protests. "Natalia just got there first. And did Katie-Rose tell you how annoyed she got? And how she made this big stink and said I'm not allowed to even talk to Natalia?"

"She said *what?*" Violet laughs, which isn't the response Yasaman is looking for. She wants Violet to say how totally out of line Katie-Rose is, telling her who she can talk to and who she can't. But all she hears is the sound of chewing.

"Violet, are you still there?" she says.

"Yeah, I'm just trying to figure out why Katie-Rose would be so jealous. Of *Natalia,* of all people."

"I know!" Yasaman says, glad Violet's finally taking it seriously.

"Do you think maybe she can't help it?" Violet asks.

"Excuse me?"

"Like, do you think maybe she doesn't *want* to act so jealous, but she can't figure out how to stop? Or it's harder than she thinks, or whatever?"

"I don't understand."

"I don't, either. Or I don't know how to explain, anyway."

"Try."

Violet exhales. "Okay. Like, forget Katie-Rose for a second. Maybe lots of people want to change things about themselves, but for whatever reason, they can't. Do you think?"

Yasaman leans against the counter, considering. Because yes, there are certainly things people *can't* change about themselves. But aren't there more things they *can* change? Otherwise, people wouldn't be people. They'd be trees, or animals.

"Like how Mr. Emerson can't change the fact that he only has one arm?" she says at last. "Is that what you mean?"

"I guess," Violet says. She sighs, and in that small sad sound, Yasaman grasps what Violet *really* means. She's referring to her mom. *Duh.*

Yasaman chooses her next words with care. "Or if someone is sick, that's something she can't change, either. She can't choose to get better just because she wants to. Because if she could, she would, right?"

"Or *he*," Violet says.

"Huh?"

"You said 'she.' But it could be a *he* who's in the hospital."

"True," Yasaman says, though she never mentioned a hospital at all.

Violet is silent. So is Yasaman.

Then Violet says softly, "I'm going to visit her today. My mom. So you're right, it *is* a 'she.'"

"Oh, Violet, I think that's awesome," Yasaman says. "When?"

"After school. I won't be able to stay long, but whatever. It's good, right?"

"It's *very* good," Yasaman says. "She must miss you so much . . . and you must miss *her* so much. I'm so happy for you!"

Violet exhales. "Thanks. I'm a little nervous. Isn't that stupid?"

"Violet, *no*. Not at all! If I hadn't seen my mom in that long, I would be totally nervous."

"And if she was, um . . ."

In a mental hospital? Yasaman thinks, filling in the end of Violet's sentence in her head. But she doesn't say it, and she doesn't make Violet say it.

"I would be incredibly nervous," she repeats.

"I just don't want to be fake," Violet says.

Yasaman is confused. "You're not. You could never be."

"Well. Anyway. Can we change the subject?"

"Of course," Yasaman says. Then she's distracted by the clop of her *ana*'s fancy shoes on the wooden floor. Her *ana* always wears fancy shoes on the bottom and beautiful makeup on the top. The rest of her, she keeps covered up.

"Time to go," her *ana* says, striding to the TV and turning off the Nick Jr. show. "We want to get there early so Nigar will have a good drop-off. Right, *küçüğüm*?"

Nigar's sweet face clouds over.

"Yaz?" Violet says. "You there?"

"I've got to go," she says abruptly.

"Oh. Um . . . okay."

Immediately, Yasaman regrets her curtness. "Sorry. It's just Nigar. I feel so bad for her." To her *ana*, she calls, "One sec, *Ana*!"

"I'll turn the van around," Yasaman's *ana* says. "Come on, Nigar. No need to look so sad."

"What's going on with Nigar?" Violet asks.

"It's Wednesday," Yasaman explains, "which means her friend Lucy won't be there. She's been having hard drop-offs on the days Lucy isn't there, and Nigar's teacher had to have a big talk with my mother. She wants Nigar to stop crying when my mother leaves."

"What?!" Violet says.

"She says it's disruptive."

Violet snorts. "That's ridiculous. What's your mom supposed to do, threaten to whip her if she gets teary?"

"I don't know," Yasaman says. She's back to feeling mixed up inside, maybe because life itself is so mixed up. Like how a person can do all sorts of things in the hope of making her day go well, such as putting on makeup or giving herself a pep talk. But the truth is, no one can control what the day brings, no matter how hard she tries.

Twenty

Camilla

"Milla, this is Stewy," Max says, holding up his hamster. "Stewy, this is Milla."

"Hi, Stewy," Milla says.

Max offers Stewy to her, and she hyperventilates and takes a step back, because she's still not sure about this hamster business. Max looks confused. Milla giggles anxiously. Max steps closer, and he is definitely and without a doubt holding Stewy out for her to take. So . . . okay. She takes him.

Eeeeek. He's warm and squirmy and snuffles in the direction of her face. He doesn't bite her, though. And his beady eyes are bright and curious, not bright and demonic. She breathes rapidly. *You're doing it,* she tells herself. *You're doing it!*

"Here's his cage," Max says, pointing to an intricate plastic affair with tunnels and spinny wheels. "See that sock? He sleeps on that sock. And here's his water bottle. I fill it every night, and he sucks on it whenever he gets thirsty."

"Cool," Milla says.

"We could let him go through his obstacle course, if you want. Do you want?"

Milla has noticed all the stuff on Max's floor. Empty Kleenex boxes with holes cut in them, wooden blocks built into archways. A piece of string hanging from the bed frame at the end of Max's bed. Dangling from the bottom of the string, a roll of orange duct tape.

"That's his tire swing," Max says. "He's supposed to jump in it and *swing,* but that hasn't happened yet."

"What are the dominoes for?" Milla asks, referring to the spiral of black-and-white rectangles a few inches from the tire swing.

"He's supposed to nudge the first one over with his

nose, and that'll trigger the rest," Max says. "It would be the first hamster-triggered domino course in the history of the world—only, that hasn't happened yet, either." Max frowns. "He either doesn't go over to the dominoes at all, or he knocks them all over at once with his big hairy body."

"He's not big and hairy." She lifts Stewy up so that she can touch her nose to his. "You're not big and hairy, are you?"

She thrusts Stewy away. "Ew! His nose is wet!"

Max laughs. "Hamsters have wet noses. It's just the way they are." But his expression is kind and open and sort of—well, sort of *delighted* with her.

Milla's never had a boy look at her like this.

"Let's put him through the course," Max suggests, taking Stewy.

"Okay," Milla says. She stands there, wondering what her role is to be. She decides it's sitting on Max's bed and watching and clapping. She steps carefully across Max's floor. She's wearing knee-high white vinyl boots with chunky heels (dangerous around Kleenex-boxes-turned-tunnels), purple leggings, and a gray sweater dress with capped sleeves and silver sparkles sewn into the fabric. She's also wearing a cute red headband with tiny felt flowers across the top. Basically, she put *a lot* of thought into her outfit.

"Ready?" Max says.

Milla perches on the end of Max's bed. She nods.

Max kneels and releases Stewy with a flourish. "Go, Stewy!"

Stewy snuffles the carpet. He lifts his head. He snuffles the air.

"Go!" Max says again. He makes shooing motions. "Move your feet!"

"Go, Stewy!!!" Milla says.

Stewy goes five inches and reaches the first obstacle: a hamster-size staircase made out of Legos. He snuffles them.

Max clutches his head. "*Up* the stairs. Up!"

Stewy puts his front paws on the bottom step. He pauses, then climbs curiously higher.

Max's eyes meet Milla's. "This is the first time he's gone this far. You must have brought him good luck!"

"I'm Stewy's good luck charm," Milla says. "Yay!"

Stewy reaches the top of the Lego staircase and, amazingly, goes down the other side. He is a hamster hero! Then he veers away from the next obstacle, which is one of the Kleenex box tunnels. Max puts him back in place.

"Through the tunnel," Milla encourages, bouncing on Max's bed. She realizes to her surprise that she wants to be in on the action, and *not* just a bystander, so she stands and hip-hops across the littered floor. She drops to her knees beside Max. "You can do it, Stewy!"

Stewy snuffles the Kleenex box.

"Go inside," Max coaches. He pats Stewy's bottom, like a gentle spank. "Go *through*."

Instead, Stewy stays right where he is, but flattens his haunches. His whiskers go back. A stain spreads around him, darkening the carpet.

"Uh-oh," Milla says. Did Stewy just . . . do what she thinks he did?

"Stewy!" Max snatches Stewy and lifts him off the floor.

More pee comes out, and Milla giggles. She's learning that hamsters are unpredictable goofballs. Who knows what Stewy's going to do next?

"No no, mister!" Max scolds, and then he yelps. Some of the pee has landed *on his jeans. Ew!*

Max lets go of Stewy, and he lands upside down on the carpet.

"Poor Stewy!" Milla cries. She's dying, she's laughing so hard.

Stewy bats his hind foot until his claws make purchase on the carpet, and then he's off and running. He's a scurrying ball of fur, and it's actually a little freaky—what if he tries to scrabble up Milla's leg?! But Max is laughing, too, and that makes it more fun than freaky.

"Help!" he says, clambering to his feet. "Hamster on the loose! Hamster on the loose!"

"There!" Milla says. The door to Max's closet isn't fully shut, and she catches sight of Stewy's hind end disappearing within.

"I'll chase him out. You grab him," Max says.

Milla crouches and holds her arms out as if she's preparing to catch a football. "Okay. Let's do it."

Max enters his closet cautiously. It's way messy, with clothes on the floor, books everywhere, and board games stacked high on a shelf. On top is a sombrero with fluffy red pompoms dangling from the rim.

"Stewy?" Max coaxes. "Come here, boy. Milla and I have to go to school, so you need to go back in your cage."

Milla tenses her muscles. She's ready to spring and grab the little guy if he appears. Or run screaming out of the room. One of the two.

Max kicks aside a blue throw pillow with a giraffe stitched on it. Next he bends at the waist and clears away some of the laundry. He lifts an unplugged lava lamp and hands it to Milla, who takes it and puts it on the floor.

There's no sight of Stewy.

"Max? Milla?" Max's mom calls. "It's about time to go, kids!"

"Coming!" Max yells over his shoulder. To Milla, he says, "Do *not* tell her Stewy's loose."

"Now, please!" his mom calls.

Max keeps searching the closet. "Come on, Stewy! Where are you?"

There's a flash of brown, and Stewy streaks out, dashing between Max's legs.

"Grab him!" Max says, but Milla is frozen. The whole

situation is exciting and dramatic and hilarious, but the freakiness is still there, adding a spine-shivery layer of anxiety. What if she lets Max down? What if she does grab Stewy, but spazzes out and lets him go?

Max loses his balance as he wades through all his junk. Stewy is mad-scrambling across the floor, and Milla is so much closer to him. *So* much.

"Don't let him get away!" Max cries, and that's it. She has to try, even if it ends in squeamish failure and total humiliation. Because Max needs her. So she lunges for Stewy, and miracle of miracles, she *catches* him. *Omigosh!*

Only he's warm and twisty and has *hamster toenails,* which scrape the pad of flesh under her thumb. It doesn't hurt, but *eeeee!* She squeals and flings Stewy away.

"Stewy!" Max cries as Stewy lands on the carpet by the toilet paper–roll tunnel. He rights himself and takes off again, not that Milla can blame him.

But *oh gosh oh gosh oh gosh.* What if she hurt him? She has to get him back. She has to make things better! She spots Stewy by the bed and dashes toward him, avoiding the obstacles on Max's floor as best she can.

"Stewy, come here, sweetie!" she begs.

Max is out of the closet. He's one step behind her.

"Do you have him?" he pants.

"Almost!" she says, leaping over the Lego staircase. She's in the air—her legs splayed, her vinyl boots gleaming—when Stewy decides to be unpredictable again. He does an abrupt about-face, darting away from the bed and straight toward Milla, and Milla has just enough time to gasp before everything shifts to slo-mo. *Because there is nothing she can do.*

She has to land. She can't stay suspended forever. And there is a snap—

And a *flump*—

And squishiness like bread, only *not* bread—

And there is blood

(red)

on her white

(but no longer *only* white)

chunky-heeled

vinyl

boot.

❄ Twenty-one ❄

Katie-Rose

When it comes to letting go of icky feelings, a good night's sleep can do wonders. Katie-Rose woke up determined to do the right thing, and do the right thing she will. She will forgive Yasaman! She will be the better person. The bigger person! No matter that she's *tiny*. When it comes to friendship, Katie-Rose has come to the conclusion that you just have to love your BFFs no matter what, especially when they're not just *B*FFs, but *F*FFs.

Anyway, Katie-Rose knows she's no saint herself. That's what she's thinking about during journal writing time. They're supposed to be writing about where they like to go to be alone, but Katie-Rose doesn't like to be alone. Ever. So she makes up her own writing prompt called "Telephone Etiquette: The Truth, the Whole Truth, and Nothing but the Truth."

It's about how she should have talked to Yasaman when Yasaman called last night. Then all their yuckiness would be over already. Instead, she made Chrissy lie and tell Yasaman she wasn't there. Chrissy wasn't pleased.

"You're not going to solve anything by avoiding her," Chrissy told her after hanging up. She cocked her head. "Unless . . . are you trying to punish her?"

"What? No!" Katie-Rose replied hotly.

"Well, she sounded sad," Chrissy said. "I'm just saying."

Scribbling away in her journal, Katie-Rose admits how lame she was not to take Yasaman's call. *Lame, lame, lame,* she writes, and *I'm going to make it up to her.* She chews on the tip of her pencil. *How? How will she make it up to her?*

Inspiration strikes! In addition to forgiving Yasaman in her head for all the Natalia stupidness, she will go that extra step and *apologize* to Yasaman for being so immature about it all. With words. Which will be hard, because it's scary to apologize to someone. It makes you feel—if you're Katie-Rose, that is—unsure of your footing, and Katie-Rose, for one, is a girl who likes to feel extremely sure of her footing at all times.

But. For a friend? For Yasaman?

I'll do it, she writes, setting her jaw. I'll do it, and I'll be brave, and so there.

She's glad when journal writing officially comes to an end. After that is morning math, and then it's snack break. Snack break means stretching and moving around and chatting, which for Katie-Rose means going over to Yasaman—who's only one desk away, though today the space between them seems huge—and saying all the stuff she wants to say before she loses her nerve.

She rises from her seat. From the corner of her eye, she sees Natalia rising from her seat, too. *Oh no you don't,* Katie-Rose thinks, sidling around her chair and quickly closing the gap between her and Yasaman. She presses her hip into the edge of Yasaman's desk to form a wall between the two of them and anyone else.

"Hi," Katie-Rose says. She wraps her arms around herself. Her hands find her armpits and worm their way in.

"Hi," Yasaman says uncertainly.

"I'm really sorry for not answering the phone last night," Katie-Rose says in a rush. She glances over her shoulder and sees that Natalia has lowered herself back into her seat, but not in a permanent-looking way. She's perched on the edge of her chair, her posture stiff.

Katie-Rose focuses on Yasaman. "I don't even know why I didn't answer, except I was mad, only maybe I was more . . . *something else* than mad. I don't know."

Yasaman regards her from under her long eyelashes. Once, at Katie-Rose's house, Katie-Rose balanced an uncooked spaghetti noodle on those lashes. She made Yasaman hold still and not blink, and she gently-gently balanced the noodle right above Yasaman's dark eyes.

Does Yasaman remember that? Katie-Rose wonders. *Of course she does,* she tells herself. *It's not like people go around balancing spaghetti noodles on their eyelashes every day of the week.*

"Anyway, I'm sorry. I shouldn't have told you what to do."

Yasaman bites her lower lip. "Well, I could have been more . . . you know. Supportive. About your speech. So I'm sorry, too."

Hearing Yasaman say this makes Katie-Rose feel a thousand times lighter. She wants to make Yasaman feel better, too, so she says, "Thanks, and I forgive you." She lowers her voice. "And personally, I think we should just blame Natalia. I *hate* her, don't you?"

Yasaman's eyebrows scrunch together. "Katie-Rose . . ."

Katie-Rose makes a face. She hates it when Yasaman says her name like that, and plus, she knows where that *Katie-Rose* is heading. She doesn't want a lecture, so says, "Fine, yes, her buttons were semi-cool. But we need to go bigger! Bolder!"

Yasaman's gaze goes to something behind Katie-Rose, and her eyes widen. Katie-Rose registers this, but not fully enough, as she is on a roll.

"Because even with Natalia's dumb buttons, nothing *changed*," she says. "Everyone still ate their Cheezy D'lites, and they're eating them again today. Just look around!"

She gestures at all the Cheezy D'lite action going on,

and her hand smacks someone's soft stomach. Natalia's soft stomach.

"Ooof," Natalia says.

Katie-Rose reddens. "Sorry."

"It'th okay," Natalia says in a tone that suggests it isn't. Then she lifts her chin. To Yasaman, she says, "I love your *hijab*. Ith it new?"

Yasaman looks pleased. "Uh-huh. My cousin gave it to me."

"It'th gorgeouth. I wish I could wear a head thcarf."

You do not, Katie-Rose thinks, wishing she'd thought to compliment Yasaman first. *You aren't Muslim, dummy.*

Natalia swivels to face her. Her headgear is like a planet. "And how are *you*, Katie-Rothe?"

"Fine," Katie-Rose says.

"I felt tho bad for you yethterday," she goes on. "When you weren't able to manage your anger? I thaid a thpecial prayer for you latht night."

Katie-Rose smiles grimly. But she isn't going to let Natalia get to her. Not today. If the situation gets too ugly, she'll use one of Chrissy's tricks for getting rid of annoying people, though she hopes it doesn't come to that.

"How nice," she says. "Tell God 'hi' for me."

"Oh, Katie-Rothe," Natalia exclaims, bringing her palms together. Her tone suggests that Katie-Rose is faking being strong, but that she, Natalia, can see right through her and, in fact, feels sorry for her.

"*Oh Katie Rose* what?! You don't need to say it like that, like I've got some kind of terminal disease."

"But you were thrown out in front of *the whole cloth*," Natalia says. "I can't even *imagine* how mortifying that mutht have been."

Katie-Rose curls her toes inside her sneakers, but keeps her smile in place. "Well, it's true that not everyone has a good imagination, but I'm sure you have lots of other skills." She widens her eyes. "Like emptying the trash. When you were the trash helper, you did an excellent job. Maybe you could be a janitor one day."

Natalia drops her concerned act. "My mom wonderth if you thkipped prethchool, and that'th why you don't know how to share."

"My mom wonders if you got dropped on your head when you were a baby, and that's why you're so annoying," Katie-Rose retorts.

"Thee?" Natalia says. "You're only thaying that to be mean, becauth you don't like me being friendth with Yathaman. You never learned to share your toyth, and now you don't know how to share, period—even the important thtuff."

Katie-Rose doesn't like where this is going, and yet she asks, irritably, "Like what?"

Natalia puts her arm around Yasaman. "Friendth, thilly."

"A friend isn't a toy."

"I know. A friend is a perthon, and you can't claim minethies on a perthon."

Minethies?

Oh. Minesies. As in a four-year-old clutching a frizzy-haired doll and twisting away when someone tries to take it, crying, "Minesies! I call minesies for today *and* tomorrow *and* the *next* tomorrow, so nanny-nanny-boo-boo!"

It's a pitch-a-fit spoiled baby word, one Katie-Rose hasn't used or thought of in a thousand years, but the awful thing is, hearing Natalia throw it at her so smugly makes her *want* to pitch a spoiled baby fit.

And why is Yasaman just standing there, Natalia's arm draped over her like a dead-rat boa? Why doesn't she fling it off like the dead rat it is?

But Katie-Rose is *not* going to let Natalia win, which means . . .

It's time for Plan Chrissy.

"Boobies from outer space!" Katie-Rose yells, making Natalia shriek and jerk violently back. Yasaman jumps, too, and from behind her desk, Ms. Perez is so startled that her fingers splay open and she drops her Starbucks cup, which lands hard on her desk, its lid bursting off and its contents spewing out. Fortunately, it was almost empty. Unfortunately, what little was left splatters Ms. Perez's rosy silk blouse.

"Girls!" she exclaims. She draws her hand to her heart, and Katie-Rose is suddenly afraid she's going to have a heart attack, right then and there.

Omigosh, I've killed my teacher, she thinks, her mouth going dry. *My teacher is going to die, and I ruined her shirt, and it's all my fault. Or maybe Chrissy's, for telling me to yell out random and embarrassing things if I need to drive people away.*

Ms. Perez doesn't die, although the spots of latte on her blouse look like dried blood. If blood were brownish, that is. She rises from her desk and strides toward the three girls. "What in heaven's name . . . ?"

Natalia gulps and scuttles away.

Weenie-head, Katie-Rose thinks, though her feet are telling her to run as well.

"Katie-Rose?" Ms. Perez says ominously.

"Omigosh, I'm so so sorry! I don't know—I was just—omigosh—and I'll *totally* buy you a new shirt, because that one's really pretty, and . . . and . . ." Why did Chrissy tell her to say the word *boobies* in public? *Boobies* is not a word people say in public! Even a second grader knows that (probably), so what was Katie-Rose thinking?

Well. She wasn't thinking, obviously. *Thanks, Chrissy.*

Ms. Perez lifts her eyebrows. Katie-Rose can't tell if she's *mad* mad, or just normal mad, but either way, Katie-Rose's anxiety builds to near bursting. She won't be able to handle it if her beloved teacher doesn't like her *again*, for the second day in a row.

Katie-Rose lifts her clasped hands in front of her the

way people do in movies when they're begging for their lives. "Please forgive me, dearest teacher who teaches me so many good things! I beseech you!"

Ms. Perez almost snorts. Katie-Rose is immensely heartened by this, and she drops to her knees and goes to her teacher, throwing her arms around Ms. Perez's calves.

"I'll never say 'boobies' at school again. I swear to you on my *life*."

"Katie-Rose . . ." Ms. Perez says. She shakes one leg, trying to dislodge her, *but she's laughing*. Maybe she doesn't want to be, but she is. She's not mad anymore!

Katie-Rose hugs Ms. Perez's legs tighter. As close as she is, she has an excellent view of Ms. Perez's stockings, which are a pale gray patterned with black roses. Roses! Another good sign!

"I like your stockings," Katie-Rose says.

"Thank you," Ms. Perez says. "Let go now, please."

"Yes, ma'am," Katie-Rose says. She releases her teacher and falls back onto her bottom.

"And now stand up, please, and return to your desk."

She gets to her feet. "Yes, ma'am."

"And, please, *I* beseech *you*. Don't ever scream 'boobies from outer space' in my classroom again." She eyeballs Katie-Rose. *"Ever."*

Titters erupt around her. Katie-Rose is too happy to care. Natalia looks like a sour pickle, and that makes Katie-Rose even happier.

"Whew," she says to Yasaman after Ms. Perez leaves the room to do what she can about her blouse. "That was close."

"You are so strange," Yasaman says. Her expression is aghast, incredulous, and admiring, all mixed together in those luminous brown eyes of hers.

"I know," Katie-Rose says. She is a buzzy ball of gladness, because not only has she fixed things with Yasaman, but she fixed that weenie-head, Natalia, too! *Ha ha ha!* Chrissy's trick *did* work!

Something pings the back of Katie-Rose's head, and she hunches over instinctively. "Ow! Hey! Who did that?"

She spots a paper football on the floor, folded tight with sharp, pointy edges. *Oh, nuh-uh,* she thinks, flabbergasted at Natalia's nerve.

Katie-Rose peeks at Natalia, who's pretending she didn't write the note. She's bent over her journal, and her tongue, pink and wet, is sticking slightly out of her mouth. Her feet are twined around the legs of her desk.

Katie-Rose sticks her own foot out and captures the note beneath the toe of her sneaker. She draws it close and unfolds it. She even smiles at Natalia—not that Natalia is looking—to say, *I can be mature, too. See?*

She smooths the note flat on her desk. A quick glance reveals messy cursive beneath some sort of picture.

Snortle heh snortle heh, she hears from the left side of the room. The *left* side of the room, which is, um, not where Natalia is. She feels a prick of foreboding, because the snortler is Preston, and the heh-heh-er is none other than Chance, who yesterday made that oh-so-hilarious jab about her brain being poisoned by Cheezy D'lites.

She shouldn't read the note. Obviously, she shouldn't read the note. Anyway, why would she? She's far too busy paying attention to their fabulous and wonderful teacher, who has returned from the teachers' lounge and has launched into a fabulous and wonderful explanation of . . . something. Definitely *something*, and whatever it is, it's fabulous, and she is not going to look down, *not* going to look down, not going to—

She looks down.

Are *your* boobies in outer space, Katie-Rose? the note says. *No wonder we've never seen them!* The picture above the words is of Saturn. With boobs.

Katie-Rose's face burns. She would punch those stupid boys if she could, or stomp on them, or pour ice water over their heads—*yeah!* Except she can't do any of those things. She can't even yell out something random like Chrissy suggested (not what she yelled before, but something else) because she's paralyzed with mortification.

Those boys! Those horrible boys! They wrote a note about—she can hardly bear to think the words—*about her very own boobs!!!*

Twenty-two

Violet

"Take out your journals." Mr. Emerson tells the class. There are groans, and Mr. Emerson says, "Hey. You think you've got it rough? Try finding true love through an internet dating service. Then we can talk. For now, *take out your journals.*"

Did Mr. Emerson just tell his class he was looking for love through an internet dating service? Violet is scandalized and delighted. She turns to share this with Milla...but Milla isn't here. Neither is Max. Maybe they're still with Stewy the hamster? She overhears Becca tell Carmen Glover that Modessa is absent, too. Violet rolls her eyes at how lame Modessa is, staying home for the second day in a row just to avoid apologizing to Cyril.

Cyril. Bleh. Violet doesn't want to think about Cyril *or* Modessa.

Mr. Emerson scrawls the free-writing prompt on the whiteboard: *Where do you go when you want to be alone?*

"Okay?" he says, facing the class. "There's a difference between being lonely and being alone by choice, and it's the second type I'm asking you to write about. You've got ten minutes, starting now."

Violet thinks for a bit, but she can't remember the last time she went somewhere to be alone on purpose. There are so many places she feels alone already, even with other people around. She could write about those places, but her list would go on forever:

Home.

School.

The girls' bathroom with its echoing tile.

The grocery store with her dad, buying individual portions of Easy Mac so that Violet can make herself a "healthy" snack when she's hungry.

She doubts Easy Mac is actually healthy, though.

Thanks to Yasaman, she's growing more aware of just how many unhealthy foods there are in the world, unhealthy foods pretending to be healthy just to make people buy them.

Cheezy D'lites, she writes in her notebook, just in case Mr. Emerson looks over. He's good about not reading their journal entries unless he's given permission, but he does want to see their pencils moving over their paper.

I need to ask Yasaman how her Snack Attack campaign is going, Violet writes. Remember to do that! And ask her if things are better with the Katie-Rose-and-Natalia situation. Maybe I should ask Katie-Rose, too? Except sometimes Katie-Rose wears me out, because she thinks only SHE has problems, when really, we all do. Every single person in the world has problems, and I bet every single person in the world feels totally alone sometimes, whether they want to be or not.

If you choose to be alone, that's one thing.

But when you're alone when you don't want to be, or when you FEEL alone even in a room full of people . . . well, like Mr. E said, then it's called "lonely."

When I think about my mom, I feel lonely.

Okay, stop that, she tells herself, because thinking about her mom at school is dangerous. That's a problem with writing. Once she starts, her ideas flow out and go all over the place, not just where they're "supposed" to go.

Is it like this for everyone? When Cyril writes in his notebook—*yes, good, switch your thoughts to Cyril, even though Cyril is bleh*—does he discover things about himself that he wouldn't have otherwise known? Or does he only write about *other* people, and does he figure out things about *other* people that he wouldn't have otherwise known?

Writing is powerful. It makes things real and shines light into shadowed corners. *Writing,* Violet realizes with a flash, *is where I go when I want to be alone.*

But Cyril . . .

He knows things about Violet that are private, and that on its own is bad and wrong. But what if he's written about those things, or is writing about them right now?

The thought makes her sick. Literally, physically, could-throw-up sick.

She has to know.

So...all right...she'll ask him. She'll ask very politely, no big deal, because if Cyril has written anything about her (or her mom), then she has a right to know, doesn't she?

She steals a glance at Mr. Emerson. He's at his desk, writing in his own journal. Whenever he gives the class a prompt, he writes about it, too, just as he pulls out a paperback and reads whenever he makes the class do silent reading.

Violet slides out of her seat and goes to Cyril. She crouches by his desk.

"Cyril," she whispers.

He looks at her. Surely he's at least a little bit surprised to see her—when has Violet, or anyone else, crept over to confer with him before?—but his dark eyes reveal nothing. His shirt today has a rainbow-colored tiger on it, and Violet's throat tightens, because tigers aren't rainbow colored. Tigers aren't rainbow colored, just like Cheezy D'lites aren't cheesy, and there are so many lies flying about that just for a second Violet sees how it could drive a person crazy. Where is the truth, if everything's a lie? Where can you be alone, if everyone is peering into your private nooks and hollows?

Then she snaps out of it, because she can, and that's the difference between her and her mom. But the burning wrongness of it remains.

"*Cyril*," Violet whispers again.

"What?" he says defensively. He folds his arms over his notebook.

"Tell me what you wrote. The other day in the principal's office, when I was on the phone."

"No."

"Tell me what you *wrote!*"

He draws back.

"Violet? Cyril?" Mr. Emerson says. "Something I should know about?"

"She wants to read my journal," Cyril says. "But that's personal, right, Mr. Emerson?"

Violet feels herself flush, because said like that it sounds creepy. The other kids titter.

"Violet, what people write in their journals is for their eyes only, unless they choose to share," Mr. Emerson says.

Violet starts to protest, but realizes it's a dead end and returns to her seat.

"*Would* anyone like to share their entry for today?" Mr. Emerson says.

Hands fly up. Not Violet's. Not Cyril's.

"Carmen, great," Mr. Emerson says. "Let's hear it."

Carmen begins. "When I want to be alone, I go to a very special place. My piano. It's a Steinway, which, if you don't know, is a very special kind of piano, and we have to get it tuned professionally twice a year. Not just by anyone, either. It has to be a special piano tuner who is familiar with Steinways. Because Steinways are so special."

She drones on. *Special special special.*

Violet's gaze slides to Cyril. *He's staring right at her.* First she sucks in a breath, heart fluttering. Then she straightens her spine and narrows her eyes.

Tell me, she commands him telepathically.

He must be telepathic, too, or maybe he's just had lots of practice communicating nonverbally. Either way, his reply comes back loud and crystal clear: *No.*

❈ Twenty-three ❈

Camilla

Milla is hiding in the bushes a little way down from Max's house. She has a tiny bit of throw-up on the corner of her mouth, but she doesn't know it. The splat of throw-up that made it all the way out of her—well, there it is on the ground, not far from where she's sitting. It's pink. She had a cherry Pop-Tart for breakfast.

That moment seems remote to her now. She sees herself in her mind as if she is another girl from another life: sitting at the table, swinging her white boots, eating the crust off her Pop-Tart to save the yummy part for last.

As she ate, she was thinking about Max. She was excited to go to his house. She was looking forward to meeting—

She squeezes shut her eyes. She pushes against them with her fists, hard enough to make flashes of light go *pop pop pop.* A stick digs into her upper thigh. *Good.*

In the hour or so she's been hiding out here, no one has emerged from Max's house. No car has pulled out of the driveway, either.

Milla isn't surprised. She wouldn't go to school, either, if her pet had just died.

And Stewy *is* dead. Milla has no doubt about that.

His small body . . .

The squish . . .

His unnatural position afterward, and on her boot, little bits of . . .

Milla heaves, but nothing comes out. Sweat beads on her forehead. She wants her moms. Either mom, though Mom Abigail is better in situations like this—only there's never before been a "situation like this" and the longer she thinks about it, the more she realizes she doesn't want to see anyone. Doesn't want to be seen *by* anyone: not her moms, not her flower friends, and certainly not Max.

She killed his hamster.

She *killed* him, and now she's a murderer, and what is she going to do???

Can she hide in these bushes forever?

No.

Can she go back to Max's house?

NO. Gosh, no. She can never see Max again.

Should she go to school? She could walk. It's not *that* far. Home is farther, but she could get there if she had to. If she could find the energy to stand up, to put one foot in front of the other and keep doing so over and over and over.

Maybe she should go to the police station—not that she knows where it is—and turn herself in. She imagines herself hunched in the corner of a cell, her arms wrapped around her shins. She'd eat mush for every meal. A steel commode would be bolted to the floor by her cot. Her only friends would be the rats that came scavenging for crumbs—that is, until they learned of her crime and decided to eat *her*.

Let them, she thinks.

Milla has thought many times of all the awful things

that could happen to her or to her family or to her friends. House fires, floods, car wrecks. Quicksand. Alligator attacks. Killer bees.

She's devised elaborate strategies for how she'll handle different emergencies, like if she and Mom Joyce are cruising down the highway in Mom Joyce's convertible, and Mom Joyce cuts her hand. Say Mom Joyce slices her thumb clean off—doesn't matter how— and a gust of wind blows it out of the convertible. It would be horrible and freaky, and Milla certainly doesn't want that to happen, but if it does, Milla knows what she'll do: First she'll tell her mom to *immediately* pull into the emergency lane. Then she'll apply pressure to the wound. She'll use her own shirt if she has to—or, better, her skirt. If she's going to end up half-naked, the bottom half is less mortifying than the top, since she doesn't yet wear a bra.

She'll speak to Mom Joyce in a gentle voice to make sure she doesn't go into shock. Then she'll say, "I'll be right back, 'kay? Keep pressing this against your cut. You're doing great."

Then she'll hop out of the car and *find that thumb.*

She'll find it in a ditch or wherever, and she'll put it in a baggie of ice, and if she doesn't have a baggie of ice, she'll dump the Coke out of her cup, keep the ice cubes, and use that. And if she doesn't have a cup of Coke ... well, she *will* have a cup of Coke. Every time she rides in Mom Joyce's convertible, she'll make sure of it. Or she'll bring an insulated lunch box, the kind with a frozen cold-pack zipped inside.

It's a decent plan, but did it serve her well this morning? No. Because the one disaster she never anticipated was What to Do if You Kill the Boy-you-like's Hamster. And now Milla can never go to school again, or see Max, or be allowed within twenty feet of small mammals.

She lies down in the shelter of the bushes, overlapping her hands beneath her head. She tucks the thumb of her right hand between her second and third fingers, an old carryover from learning not to suck her thumb. She holds her thumb like this when she goes to sleep, and usually it comforts her.

Not today.

Twenty-four

Yasaman doesn't yet pray five times a day like her parents do. She will when she's older, but kids don't have to, and her parents have assured her that she can be a good Muslim without sneaking off to the girls' bathroom throughout the day and bowing toward Mecca. (Which is lucky, as the girls' room has no windows, and Yasaman's not even sure which direction Mecca is.)

But today she gives prayer-at-school a shot, maybe because of Natalia's earlier comment about praying for Katie-Rose. Yasaman would like to pray for Katie-Rose *and* for Natalia, and for herself as well, because the

Katie-Rose-Natalia-Yasaman triangle (which shouldn't even be a triangle!) still feels like a tangled mess. Katie-Rose might think everything's back to being easy-peasy-lemon-squeezy, but Yasaman's not there yet. She's not even close.

She goes to the bathroom at the end of the school day and waits while a kindergartner named Sierra washes her hands. She helps Sierra with the paper towel dispenser, which is tough to crank, and Sierra says, "I'm only using one, because I care about trees."

"That's great," Yasaman says.

"I know," Sierra says, and Yasaman smiles. Sierra's certainty reminds her of Katie-Rose, who also has a high opinion of herself and her opinions. But Katie-Rose has a vulnerable side, too, which only her flower friends see. Like on Sunday, when Milla was late getting to Katie-Rose's house, and Katie-Rose couldn't stop fretting about it. She tried to pass it off as grumpiness, but Yasaman knew better.

Yasaman wets a paper towel and lightly wipes her face and behind her ears. Then she washes her hands and her arms, up to her elbows. While she cleans her body, she focuses her thoughts on cleansing her soul as well, so that she can reach out to Allah with a pure spirit.

When she's done with that part of the ritual, she retreats to the farthest stall and locks the door. She thinks of her *baba* and the special room he prays in. When she was little, she sometimes prayed beside him, sitting on her knees and pressing her forehead to the carpet. Other times—she knows this from hearing family stories—she would jump on top of him as he prayed, making him go *oomph.*

Now that she's older, she's no longer allowed to pray with him in his special room. She wouldn't get in trouble, exactly, but since she's a young lady, it's better for her to pray with her *ana.*

Alone in the bathroom, she closes her eyes and silently thanks God for the many blessings in her life. She means it, too. So much.

Then she prays about what's bothering her. Normally, she'd go to her flower friends with this sort of thing, but today they weren't much help. At lunch, Violet wasn't in the mood to talk, and Milla wasn't there. Violet said she guessed she was home sick.

Oh no, Yasaman thought when she heard that, because that meant Milla must have had to cancel her plans with Max. Poor Milla kept having bad luck in that department.

With neither Violet nor Milla available for a good heart-to-heart, that left Katie-Rose. But Yasaman couldn't ask Katie-Rose for help with her problem, because Katie-Rose was the problem. *Is* the problem. *Blegh.*

Please, she says to Allah, trying to communicate the depth of her need with that one word. She wants to say more, but she's unsure how to put it, because no doubt Allah has bigger things to worry about than the feud between Katie-Rose and Natalia, and how Yasaman feels trapped in the middle.

Yasaman's loyalty lies with Katie-Rose (of course!), but the way Katie-Rose has been acting makes her extremely uncomfortable. Her *baba* has taught her that according to the Quran, you shouldn't treat people badly, even your enemies, and you shouldn't stay mad at anyone for more than three days. But Katie-Rose first got mad at Natalia on Monday, when Natalia found her sticking police tape over the snack cabinet. She stayed mad all through Tuesday, and she's obviously still mad today. Mad enough to say she hated her, and to yell "boobies from outer space" at her.

(And, um, *boobies from outer space*??? What was *that* all about?)

Yasaman tries to find a place of stillness inside of her. *Please help me be a good friend to Katie-Rose without being a bad friend to Natalia,* she prays. *Not that Natalia and I are even friends, exactly. But please help me be kind to her anyway, and help Katie-Rose be kind, too.*

Her thoughts drift to Modessa and Quin and how mean they are to almost all the fifth-grade girls—and to some of the boys as well. (Case in point: Cyril.) Not long ago, Modessa and Quin were especially mean to Katie-Rose, so Katie-Rose knows what it's like to be on the other end of the stick. Shouldn't she put the stick down, then, and not treat people that way herself?

Please help everyone just be nice to each other, Yasaman concludes. *And please help Milla feel better, and please help Violet have a good visit with her mom.* She squeezes her eyelids closed extra hard. *And, um, thanks.*

With a renewed sense of purpose, she leaves the

bathroom and seeks out Natalia. She finds her in the commons, because that's where the aftercare kids meet, and Natalia stays for aftercare almost every day. Yasaman has never stayed for aftercare. She's supposed to be outside waiting for her *ana,* who will be in a hurry since they're having dinner at her aunt's house.

"Come, come, come!" she'll call to Yasaman when she spots her. Nigar will be buckled into her booster seat already, because the preschoolers get out earlier than everyone else. "We have *katmer* to make, and also almond custard. I need your help, *küçüğüm!*"

But Yasaman can see the carpool line from the commons, and her *ana*'s minivan is nine or ten back. She's got a little time.

She goes over to Natalia, who's sitting alone at a table, working on her homework.

"Natalia?" she says.

Natalia looks up. "Yathaman! Are you thtaying for aftercare? Do you want to do your homework with me? And *omigosh*"—her face grows bigger, somehow—"have you *heard*?!"

Yasaman isn't here for the gossip. And she only has a

few minutes to say what she wants to say. Still, she can't help asking: "Heard what?"

"Well," Natalia says importantly. "I've been looking for you ever thince afternoon break. That'th when it happened, you thee, and, of course, you were the firtht perthon I wanted to tell."

The way Natalia leans forward tells Yasaman that she's in for a long, detailed story, and Yasaman inwardly groans. She doesn't have time for a long, detailed story.

"Wait. Natalia—"

"It began when I found a pen by the water fountain," Natalia proclaims. "I'm ninety-thix perthent pothitive it'th mine, becauth I had one ethactly like it latht year. It had the thame fluffy pink featherth and *every*thing."

"That's great, Natalia. But—"

"I'm not done! Becauth Ava thaw me pick it up—the pen—and she wath like—"

"Natalia, *please*," Yasaman interrupts. She's firmer than usual, and Natalia breaks off in surprise. She blinks at Yasaman, and Yasaman stands as tall as she can.

"I just wanted to say that I'm sorry about Katie-Rose," Yasaman says.

"You are?" Natalia says.

"I am. For how she's been treating you."

"Ohhhh." Natalia's features shift, and a less trusting person might describe her expression as cagey. But Yasaman, who always tries to think the best of people, decides surely she's mistaken.

"All I wanted—all I *ever* wanted—wath to help with the Thnack Attack," Natalia says.

"I know," Yasaman says.

"But Katie-Rothe jutht doethn't like me. I don't know why. And thometimeth? Honethtly? I think she might be clinically inthane, or why elthe would she thay the thingth she doeth?"

Yasaman grows wary. Yes, she thinks Katie-Rose was wrong to yell "boobies from outer space" at Natalia, but Katie-Rose is still her BFF, and she doesn't want to say anything that could be misinterpreted. Plus, there's Violet's mom to think about. Katie-Rose *isn't* clinically insane, and Natalia knows it. But some people really are, so to say that as an insult is wrong. Like using the r-word to describe someone who does something dumb.

Natalia builds up steam. "Do you know how long

I thpent on thothe buttonth? I'm not complaining, but jutht coming up with the thlogan took *forever*."

Why Snackrifice? Yasaman thinks, envisioning the shiny white buttons. "It's a really good slogan," she says truthfully.

"You mean it? Becauth I worked my butt off to come up with it. Wath it hard? Abtholutely. But I jutht kept trying, and if that meant thtaying up late and getting a migraine, too bad."

"You got a migraine?"

"Of courth it *had* to be the blinding kind. Have you ever had one?"

Yasaman fidgets. She looks over her shoulder to see where her *ana* is in the pickup line.

"But I wath like, *mind over matter*. I refuthed to give up, not till I conthidered every option and drained every thingle brain thell to come up with the perfect one."

"Oh," Yasaman says. "Um, wow."

Natalia works her jaw to adjust her headgear. Her chin juts out, then comes back in. She smiles. "Anyway, I'm glad you like it."

"I do."

"Katie-Rothe doethn't, though. She hateth it."

"Oh, I don't think so. I'm sure she doesn't *hate* it."

Natalia gives Yasaman a long look. "Well, maybe she jutht hateth *me*."

"No, Natalia, she doesn't," Yasaman protests.

"She thaid she did. She told me herthelf."

Yasaman flounders. Yes, Katie-Rose told Yasaman she hated Natalia . . . but would she really tell Natalia that? To her face?

"I try not to let it get to me," Natalia says. Her voice trembles. "I mean, she'th inthecure, obviouthly. She'd have to be to order me not to talk to you, right?"

"That was wrong of her," Yasaman says. She's upset with Katie-Rose all over again for putting her in this position. "And she's not my boss, obviously, because here I am talking to you."

"And later, when you weren't there . . ." Natalia doesn't finish. She glances about nervously and says, "Never mind."

Yasaman's stomach hurts. "Well. Okay. So I guess I'll see you tomorrow?"

"She thaid I'm not good enough to be your friend,"

Natalia says in a rush. "That you agree, only you're too nithe to thay tho."

Yasaman breaks out in a cold sweat. This is her first ever time to experience such a thing, but here it is: cold sweat on her spine, at her hairline, under her arms.

"Natalia, I *never* said that. I promise."

Natalia tilts her head as if she's trying to decide if she can believe her. "But if you didn't . . . why would Katie-Rothe thay you did?"

"I don't *know*," Yasaman says. Her heart is pounding.

Miraculously, Natalia lets her off the hook. "Well, I'm jutht glad it ithn't true. I didn't think it wath, becauth it jutht doethn't thound like you, you know?" She frowns. "I don't think Katie-Rothe should lie, though."

Yasaman shakes her head. "No, no one should." She gets an idea. "What if it was a mistake? I bet it was! I'll call her and ask her, as soon as I get home."

"You're thweet," Natalia says. "But it'th not the firtht time Katie-Rothe hath been hateful." She smiles bravely. "I'll thurvive, jutht ath long ath she doethn't turn you againtht me."

"But I'm sure it was a misunderstanding," Yasaman says. "I'll talk to her."

She turns to leave, but Natalia grabs her forearm. Yasaman looks down at Natalia's pale fingers. She lifts her head, confused.

"Really, you don't need to worry about me," Natalia says. There's something glittery in her eyes, and her expression has taken on a new intensity. "The perthon you need to worry about ith Milla."

Yasaman furrows her brow. "Milla?"

"That'th what I thtarted to *tell* you. About the pen? And how Ava thaid I wath lying about it being mine, even though I never lie?"

"What does the pen have to do with Milla?" Yasaman asks. She pulls her arm from Natalia's grasp. "Never mind. I have to go, or my mom's going to be mad."

"No, you need to hear thith," Natalia says. "I knew Ava wath wrong, but *jutht in cathe* I dethided to give it to Pam to put in the lotht-and-found. And while I wath at the offithe, do you know who I thaw?"

"Yasaman!" calls Ms. Perez, poking her head into the commons. "Your mom's here, cutie!"

234

"Um, okay!" Yasaman says. "Be right there!" She turns back to Natalia. "Speak. *Now*. And use fast words, please."

"It wath Max. Hith mom brought him in late." Natalia watches Yasaman's face, and Yasaman gets a bad feeling. "And after he went to clath, do you want to know what hith mom told Pam?"

"Yes," Yasaman says. "Just tell me!"

"His hamthter died."

"Stewy?"

"Ith Thtewy the hamthter's name?"

"*Yes*, his name's Stewy. He *died*?"

Natalia nods gravely. So gravely, in fact, that it seems wrong. As if her graveness is covering up something exciting, or something *not* exciting that Natalia finds exciting anyway.

She drops her voice. "*Milla killed him*. She *thtepped* on him. She thtepped right on him, and . . ." She widens her eyes. "*Thquish*."

Oh no, Yasaman thinks. She presses her hand over her mouth.

"And now he'th dead, and that'th why Max wath late, becauth he wath *grieving*. That'th what hith mom thaid. And that'th why Milla didn't come to thchool at all, I bet."

"But . . . she's sick," Yasaman says, feeling far away in her head. "She was absent because she's sick."

"I don't think tho," Natalia says.

Ms. Perez pops into the building again. "Yasaman, come on. Your mom's waiting."

Yasaman tries her best to pull herself back to the moment. "Natalia, how many people know about this?"

"Jutht you," Natalia says.

"Oh, thank goodness."

"I'm not a gothip-thpreader," Natalia says piously.

"I know, I know." Yasaman chews her bottom lip. "I think we should promise not to tell anyone else, okay?"

"Not even Katie-Rothe and Violet?"

"Well, yes *them*, because they're Milla's best friends. But no one else."

"Jutht you and me and Violet and Katie-Rothe," Natalia says.

"Right."

"Jutht uth five."

"Yes, that's right," Yasaman agrees impatiently. She

needs to go to Milla, and she needs to go now. Only—*ag*.
She can't. She has to help her *ana* make the *katmer*, and
her *ana* isn't the type of mother to understand why a
dead hamster is more important.

Please-oh-please let Violet or Katie-Rose still be here,
she prays as she rushes out of the building. She hopes
Allah is listening.

Twenty-five

Violet

*T**here's nothing like the death of a hamster** to put things in perspective,* Violet thinks. Yasaman caught her right as she was climbing into her dad's car and told her the whole gruesome tale. Violet feels sick with it, and worried for Milla, but she *can't* cancel on her mom again, even though this excuse is by far the most legitimate of all that have come before.

So she uses her dad's cell phone to call Katie-Rose. She gets Katie-Rose's answering machine, and she tells her about Stewy and Max and that that's why Milla was absent. She ends with, "You have to go see her, Katie-

Rose. You're her only hope. And tell her we *all* love her, okay?"

Her dad arches his eyebrows as she hands him back his phone.

"Want to talk about it?" he asks.

She shakes her head. Then, worried she may have hurt his feelings, she says, "No offense. I just …" *I just can't handle any more drama, and if I talk about it, I might cry.* "I just need to chill out a little."

Her dad puts his hand on her leg and squeezes. She looks at his profile and thinks what a strong, handsome father she has. She's very lucky, and all the bad stuff that's going on doesn't take that away. Oddly, it makes her even more aware of her good fortune. She puts her hand on top of her dad's and squeezes back.

For the rest of the drive, they're quiet. Her dad's iPod is hooked up to the car stereo, and a mellow, raspy song plays through the speakers. Violet lets the music carry her away, though she never strays very far. *Mom. Cyril. Milla. Mom. Cyril. Milla.*

If Katie-Rose checks for phone messages right away, she could already be on her way to Milla's house. Tonight,

Violet will call and check in on Milla herself. She knows Yasaman will, too.

Violet leans her forehead against the cool glass of the window. It's beautiful outside, though not as beautiful as Atlanta. In Atlanta, the leaves would be changing color: The forests would hum with russets and golds and deep dark purples. But here in Thousand Oaks, land of perpetual summer, the thousands of oak leaves are as green and vibrant as ever.

What about her mom? Has she changed here in California, in this special California hospital? And if so ... how?

Violet's dad pulls into the gated driveway of the Mental Marriott. Violet's heart pounds, and her accelerating pulse kicks her thoughts into high gear, too:

Mom ... Cyril ... Milla ...

and Stewy, dead forever ...

Some things can be changed, but some things can't ...

like death ...

like Mr. Emerson's arm ...

but an arm isn't a leaf isn't a mother isn't a hamster—

"We're here, Boo," Violet's dad says.

Violet reaches across her seat and grabs her dad's hand. His fingers close around hers.

"It's going to be okay," he tells her.

Violet nods. The back of her neck tingles.

"She's still your mom. She'll *always* be your mom." He squeezes her hand, and his love for her says, *And I will always be your dad.*

Climbing out of the car isn't easy, but she does it. Her heart goes *bum bum bum* as she walks through the hospital's front doors, but she doesn't faint or die or anything.

Her dad talks to an old man sitting behind the information desk. The old man is wearing a name tag that says HOSPITALITY VOLUNTEER. He gives Violet's dad two badges, and Violet's dad thanks him and leads Violet to the elevators. There are three of them. He pushes the "up" arrow, then points at the middle elevator and says, "I'm betting on that one."

Violet tries to smile. It's an old game Violet's family plays, though they haven't in a long time.

"Um, I guess I'll take that one," Violet says, indicating the elevator on the far left.

Violet wins.

Is it a sign?

They get off on the fifth floor. Violet's dad checks in at the nurses' station, and a grumpy-looking woman comes around the desk and escorts them to a heavy-duty door with a small glass pane at the top, crosshatched with faint lines.

Breathe, Violet tells herself as the woman inserts a key card into a slot. *You are the cosmos, and the cosmos is you.*

She is surprised by that last thought, as she doesn't know where it came from. She laughs nervously.

"Sweetie?" her dad says. "You all right?" He has stepped through the door without her, and now it's Violet's turn to cross the threshold between "unlocked" and "locked." Because yes, her mother lives in a locked ward. That is the awful truth of it. Not because she's dangerous or anything—Violet imagines a knife-wielding psycho, and immediately banishes the image—but because that's just the rule. All the psychiatric patients are in the locked ward. It's for their own safety, her dad has explained. And any patients who might physically harm someone in a knife-wielding way are kept somewhere else, anyway.

She joins her dad. He takes her hand.

The nurse in charge of the key card says, "Forty minutes," and then she leaves, pulling the door shut behind her. *Violet is now locked in.*

But as her eyes flit about, she is surprised by how cheerful the ward is.

It's not so bad here, she thinks. The walls are a pale orange—Yasaman's favorite color—and broad windows provide lots of natural light. Not far from the door is a second nurses' station, and past that is a sitting area with a flat-screen TV and comfy-looking sofas and chairs.

Violet spots a young woman sitting on one of the sofas, her knees pulled to her chest. She's wearing a nightgown. She's rocking and murmuring, despite the fact that there's no one beside her.

But there are no rats. There are no roaches. The nurse who let them in was crabby, but the nurse in here is young and pretty and says, "Hi, Theo." She smiles at Violet. "And you must be Violet. I'm Faye. Nice to meet you."

"Um, hi," Violet says.

"Your mom can't wait to see you." She gestures at a hall that connects to the sitting room. "She's in her room."

Violet looks at her dad. He squeezes her hand and leads her to room 513. Violet knows she's being silly, but she wishes it were a different number: 505 or 510.

"I'll let you two have some time alone," her dad says in a low voice. "I know it's been a long time . . . well . . . since . . ." He swallows. "It's fine, though. It's fine."

Violet bows her head. Hotness spreads through her.

Her dad raps on the door, twists the knob, and cracks it open. His body blocks Violet's vision, but her mother is *here*, so close. Just feet away.

"Hey, hon," her dad says to her mom. "Violet's here to see you."

Violet hears a gasp, and the shuffling of sheets, and then the rapid pad of footsteps. The door flies open. *"Violet?"* Her mother draws her hand to her mouth. Her dark eyes shine. "Oh, Violet! *Oh,* how I've missed you!"

And then she's hugging her, and it doesn't matter that Violet's vision has suddenly gone blurry, because she's smushed up against her mother's hospital gown anyway. *And it really is her mother.* Violet is overwhelmed by her scent, her warmth, the wonderful feeling of her mother's arms around her, holding her tight tight tight.

A sound squeezes out of Violet, and her mother releases her.

"Oh, baby, did I hurt you?" she says, worry creasing her brow.

Of course she did. The hurt lives behind Violet's ribs, and it may never go away. But it's less now than it was yesterday. Less than it was five minutes ago.

"No," Violet lies. She feels older, and sad-happy, but also at peace. For now. She wants to tell her mom this, but she doesn't have the words.

Violet's mother pulls her back into an embrace, and Violet soaks up every bit of her. Even a little can go a long way, if she lets it.

Twenty-six

I'm biking over to Milla's!" Katie-Rose calls to her mom after listening with growing distress to Violet's phone message. "I'll be back!"

She leaves before her mom can tell her *no*. She wheels her bike out of the garage, climbs on, and pushes off, glancing at Max's house as she pedals past. Inside that house, a tragedy occurred. A life was snuffed. And yet a casual observer would have no idea. Shouldn't there be candles in the windows? A makeshift memorial, like when someone dies in a car accident on the highway, and people place teddy bears and flowers and posters at the spot where their loved one died?

But, no. Everything looks exactly as it always does, from the house's stucco exterior to the lushly landscaped yard. Same stone bench by the juniper tree. Same wild currant plants, which hummingbirds flock to for their nectar. Same flowering sage bushes, which Katie-Rose loves the smell of, but which Max thinks smell weird, like skunk.

She's past Max's house and all the way to the end of the block before a mysterious detail registers in her mind. She saw it, but thought nothing of it until now, when its subtle wrongness clicks into place.

It had to do with the sagebrush that stretches along the sidewalk in front of Max's house. There's a neighborhood cat named Zero who likes to hide in those bushes, his tail twitching as he watches the hummingbirds. But Zero is black, and what Katie-Rose saw was white. White and shiny. She makes a U-ie and cruises slowly back, squinting into the dense sagebrush.

There. A shiny white boot lying on its side. And *there,*

next to it, its mate—only not as uniformly shiny and white. Splattered with rust-colored spots. Like coffee. Like blood.

Katie-Rose feels the punch of it in her gut. She swings her leg over the frame of her bike, coasts to a stop, and jumps off. She abandons her bike and approaches the hedge.

She squats when she reaches the spot where the boots are. They're not in plain sight; they're tucked in among the twisty branches. And yes, they're Milla's. Katie-Rose would know them anywhere. And the rust-colored spots on the right boot . . . well. Katie-Rose stays balanced on her haunches, focusing her thoughts on Stewy and saying good-bye to him in her mind.

Katie-Rose's quads burn, but she holds the position a little longer, because it seems like the right thing to do. Then she gives a short nod and shifts forward onto her knees. She reaches through the branches and grabs the first boot, the one that's still white. She can't leave Milla's boots here, after all. She tosses it over her shoulder and goes back for boot number two. This one's farther in, and she has to crawl forward on her tummy, turning her head to the side so she doesn't poke her eyes out.

Blindly she pats the dirt. "Come on, boot," she mutters. "Come to Mommy."

The boot snuffles, and Katie-Rose yelps and scrambles frantically backward. *Because boots don't snuffle.* So what did? A raccoon? A rat? A wild pig, rooting for truffles?!

"Hey!" she says. She fumbles for the first boot and uses it to whack the bushes. "Get out of there, you . . . thing!"

The thing snuffles again. It's actually a very human-sounding snuffle, and the base of Katie-Rose's spine tingles. She crawls cautiously forward and peers into the shadowed network of leaves and branches.

Milla lifts her hand. Her eyes are puffy, and her hair is a mess. There are twigs in it. *Twigs.*

"Milla?" Katie-Rose says. "Why are you hiding in the bushes?"

Milla shrugs.

"Well . . . get out!"

Milla shakes her head.

Katie-Rose briefly closes her eyes. A remarkable calm descends upon her, and when she opens her eyes, she knows she was born to be here at this very moment. She was born for other things, too—she has many many moments of greatness ahead of her—but right now her job is to get her shoeless, tearstained friend out of the sagebrush.

She gazes levelly at Milla and extends her hand. "Come on."

Milla starts crying. "I killed St-stewy! I st-stepped on him!"

"I know. It's okay."

"Nuh-uh, I *killed* him! It's not okay at all!"

"I know. You're right. But I need you to get out of those bushes now." She beckons with her fingers. "Come on. You can do it."

Milla wants to, Katie-Rose can tell. If she's been here all day—*omigosh*, she has, hasn't she? Well, she's got to be starving. She's got to be desperate for a bathroom, too. Unless she peed in the sagebrush?

Not the time to ask.

"Here's what's going to happen," Katie-Rose says. "You're going to come out of there—come on, take my hand—and we're going to have a memorial service for Stewy."

Milla *does* take Katie-Rose's hand. Milla's is cold, while Katie-Rose's is warm.

"But Stewy's dead," Milla wails. "And I don't know what Max did with . . . his body. And I'm not going to ask!"

Katie-Rose twines her fingers around Milla's. "Then we'll bury your boots."

Milla sob-laughs. Katie-Rose tugs at her, and she scoots inch by inch over the dirt. When she's nearly there, she lets go of Katie-Rose and crawls out into the open air.

"You're a mess," Katie-Rose remarks. She lifts her eyebrows, deciding not to tell her that there's actually a roly-poly making a home in her tangled blonde hair. Instead, she says, "I mean, wow. I don't think I've ever seen you so . . . nature-girl-y."

Milla glances fearfully at Max's house. "I need to get out of here," she whispers.

"Of course." Katie-Rose gets to her feet and pulls Milla up. "We'll go to my house. We'll get you cleaned up. I'll make you hot cocoa, okay?"

Milla takes a shuddery breath. "I should probably call Mom Joyce and Mom Abigail, too."

"Yep." She aims Milla toward her house and gives her a push. "You go on. I've got to get my bike, and . . . yeah. But I'll be right there."

"You promise?"

"I promise."

She watches Milla dart across the street. She waits until her mom has ushered Milla in—with a hug and a look of concern—and then she worms her arm back into the sagebrush and grabs the second boot. When she pulls it out, a bramble scratches her forearm.

She climbs awkwardly onto her bike, using one hand to steer and the other to hold the boots. In the garage, she shoves the boots behind a grass seeder her dad never uses. She starts to leave, then returns and throws an oil-stained burlap blanket over them, just in case.

If some day in the future Milla decides she does

want to bury her boots—whether it's days, weeks, or months from now—Katie-Rose will help her. She'll even volunteer to give the eulogy. And if that's not something Milla chooses to do, maybe Katie-Rose will bury them herself, to pay her respects to Stewy.

Thursday, September 22

Twenty-seven

Camilla

Milla wakes up in the middle of the night after dreaming of spiky things and crumbly Vanilla Wafers and being trapped in mud, squelchy, greedy mud that sucked at her bare feet and tried to pull her under.

She sits up in bed and shivers. It's dark out, which means it's still night, which makes her pull the blankets tighter around her. She hates being awake in the middle of the night. Hates having to fall back asleep by herself, and anyway, she never can. It's too freaky.

But when she looks at her "Fatally Addicted to Cute"

clock, it says five thirty, which means it's *not* night, but the next day. And not only that, but later than five A.M. the next day—and *that* means she doesn't have to be alone. The rule is that after five o'clock, if she absolutely can't get back to sleep, she's allowed to go crawl in with Mom Joyce and Mom Abigail.

She feels a gut-wrenching twist of relief. She slips out of bed and tiptoes downstairs to her parents' room. She pads over to Mom Abigail's side of the bed and whispers, "Mom? Can I get in?"

Mom Abigail, who sleeps through beeping alarms but wakes up at the least little Milla-sound, groggily opens her eyes. She squints at her clock.

"Sweetie, it's two in the morning," she says.

"It is?" Milla looks at her mom's clock. Sure enough, it is. She must have flipped the two into a five, up in her own room.

"Go back to bed, sweetie," Mom Abigail says, closing her eyes and blindly patting Milla. She draws her arm back into the warmth of the covers and pulls the covers up under her chin. "Love you."

"Love you, too," Milla says.

She doesn't leave.

Mom Abigail cracks one eye.

"Can I get in anyway?" she asks.

"Sweetie, you know the rule," Mom Abigail says. "Otherwise, you'd be down here every night. You've got your own bed, babe."

But it doesn't have you guys in it, Milla thinks. It really *is* dark, here and in the rest of the house. Especially upstairs. How could she have thought it was five thirty?

Mom Abigail sighs, scoots farther toward the middle of the bed, and lifts up the baby pink comforter.

Milla happily crawls in. She wiggles her spine up against Mom Abigail, and Mom Abigail wraps around her. On the other side of the bed, Mom Joyce shifts and makes a funny sleep-noise that makes both Milla and Mom Abigail quietly giggle.

"That woman, I swear," Mom Abigail whispers. She strokes Milla's hair. Milla loves it when her mom does that. She's warm and cozy now, like a baby bunny snuggled safely in its bunny den. *Only—*

She tenses.

"What's wrong, baby?" her mom asks.

Baby. Baby bunnies. Stewy. It all comes back.

She burrows her face into her mom's pillow. Her words come out muffled. "I'm feeling sad about Stewy."

"Mmm," her mom says. "That's normal, Mills. You'll probably feel sad for a while." She keeps stroking Milla's hair, separating the strands and gently untangling them. "You didn't mean to, though, baby."

"I know."

"And Max knows you didn't mean to."

"I know." *No, he doesn't.*

"Everyone knows you didn't mean to. You're going to survive this, sweetie."

Well, no, probably not, Milla thinks.

After Milla got home this afternoon, there'd been a lot of talking. Mom Abigail and Mom Joyce talked to Milla, of course, telling her how much they loved her and how she wasn't a bad person and how she should never *ever* skip school again. *Ever.* Then Mom Abigail got on her phone and talked to Max's mom, and Mom Joyce got on her phone and talked to Ms. Westerfeld, the principal of Rivendell, who said she would talk to Mr. Emerson, Milla's teacher. The grown-ups were kind and understanding, though firm about the skipping-school part. They all said everything would be okay.

But grown-ups say stuff like that.

Her mom's breathing slows. Her hand drifts from Milla's hair to the base of her neck, where it nestles in like a small animal, like a—

No, Milla tells her brain.

She closes her eyes. She listens to her moms' sleeping sounds, and she tries to feel sleepy herself. She really tries.

Her eyelids pop open.

She moves Mom Abigail's hand out of the way and flops onto her back. Then to her other side, so that she's facing her mom. She squirms to get her pajamas unwrinkly beneath her, and Mom Joyce makes a *mmphy-grummphy* noise.

"Whoever's wiggling, stop," she says grouchily.

Milla holds still. She tries again to *fall asleep*. It's not happening, though. It's just not. In order to keep her eyes shut, she has to scrunch her forehead muscles, and then, when she tries to unscrunch her forehead, her eyes fly open.

It's more than scrunchy muscles, of course. It's Stewy, and Max, and knowing she's a terrible person who brings sadness wherever she goes.

Grrrrrr! Think about something else! she commands herself. Think about . . . about Yasaman and her Snack Attack. That's a good thing, right? A way of making the world better instead of sadder? Not that she's contributed much to the campaign other than the Jelly-Yums, which weren't a hit.

She scratches her nose. She wants to come up with something *big*. But what? To come up with more ideas, she needs to know more about the problem, so she carefully-carefully turns over and scooches toward the edge of the bed. Her Mom Abigail's iPhone is on the bedside table, plugged in and charging, and Milla reaches for it. She holds it low so its screen light won't wake anyone. She goes to Google and types "trans fats," "Cheezy D'lites," and "badness" into the search bubble.

She'll start with that. If she doesn't find anything, she'll keep searching, even if it means staying up till dawn.

Twenty-eight

Katie-Rose also gets up early on Thursday, though not as early as Milla. She gets up at seven instead of seven thirty and does a vigorous, two-minute stretching-and-jogging-in-place routine. Then she gets dressed: denim miniskirt, a T-shirt with a daisy on it, and mismatched leg warmers with pompoms at the top. It's a power outfit, and Katie-Rose has chosen it with care, knowing that Milla is going to need every ounce of her strength and support today.

Milla's going to need all her flower friends today.

Katie-Rose hopes that Natalia, for once, has the sense to simply stay out of the way.

Katie-Rose is ready before her mom or brothers, so she goes outside for a moment of solitude. Only it's not solitude if there's another person with you, or near you, or across the driveway from you, sitting in a forlorn way on his front steps.

"Hi, Max," she says, going over to him. She reaches out to touch his shoulder, then feels awkward and doesn't. She puts her hands behind her back. "I'm really sorry about Stewy."

"Thanks," Max says.

"Milla didn't mean to do it, you know."

Max nods.

"Was he . . . in pain?"

"I don't think so," Max says. "My mom called a friend of hers who's a doctor, and the doctor said Stewy probably died right away. The doctor wasn't there, so she couldn't say for sure, but . . . yeah."

"Oh."

Max swallows. "But his legs kept moving. Afterward."

"What?" Katie-Rose says, alarmed.

"My mom's friend said that sometimes happens, though. Because of brain signals still being sent out. But it doesn't mean Stewy was still alive, or that he was suffering."

Katie-Rose is suffering just hearing this, and also from seeing Max so wrecked. She hesitates, then asks, "Are you mad? At Milla?"

"No," Max says. Katie-Rose can see he's telling the truth, and she feels ashamed for every petty thing she's ever done.

"I called her," Max goes on, "but she wouldn't come to the phone."

"Well, she'll be at school," Katie-Rose says. "You can talk to her there."

"Yeah. But if you see her first, will you tell her?" He lifts his head and meets Katie-Rose's eyes. "That I know she didn't mean to kill Stewy, and that I'm not mad?"

Katie-Rose's throat tightens.

"Katie-Rose!" her mom calls. "Come on, sweetie!"

"I've got to go," she says. "But of course I'll tell her."

She walks back to her own house, promising silently to be a better person from this day forth. She knows now how fragile life is. It's stupid to get worked up over small annoyances, and so she won't, not ever again.

Twenty-nine

Camilla

The only way Milla gets through morning math is by silently going over what she learned on the internet at three A.M. Oh, and also by putting up an invisible wall between her and Max. She feels him looking at her, but she cannot and does not look back.

Factory farms, she says to herself. *Cramped cages, genetically altered chickens, mean people who work at slaughterhouses.* Not everybody would connect Cheezy D'lites to such horrors, but Milla discovered that Cheezy D'lites are just one small part of the problem. The real evil lies with Happy Healthy Farms, the company that makes Cheezy D'lites. There is *nothing* happy or healthy about Happy Healthy Farms.

Milla is not a girl who usually fights for things, but today she will, one way or another. Yasaman's cause is worth fighting for. Animal rights are worth fighting for. And in Milla's mind, though she can't exactly explain it, the Snack Attack has morphed into something bigger: a way to say *sorry* to Stewy.

Someone is saying Milla's name. It's Violet. Milla emerges from her fog and sees the other fifth graders lined up by the door that leads to the playground, bouncing off one another with the hyperness of imminent freedom.

"It's morning break," Violet says, standing over Milla.

"Right," Milla says.

Violet tugs on her arm. "So get up."

But Milla resists. Other than Violet and herself, only one other person isn't goofing off with the other kids. He's at the end of the line. His socks are pulled up too high as always.

Violet follows Milla's gaze. "Oh," she murmurs, releasing Milla's arm. She waits with Milla until everyone has left the room, including Max. *Then* they go outside.

Milla sticks close to Violet and says, "We need to find Yasaman and Katie-Rose. I have something important to tell you guys. It's about the Snack Attack."

"Seriously?" Violet says "I mean, wow. I mean, I wouldn't have thought . . . given everything that happened..."

"Uh-huh," Milla says to make her stop.

Milla spots Yasaman near the swing set. Yasaman comes forward and immediately gives Milla a hug.

"Milla..." she begins.

"Thanks," Milla says, gently leaning away from the embrace. "Where's Katie-Rose? We need Katie-Rose."

"Here I am," Katie-Rose says, hurrying over. "What's up?"

"So I've found out some stuff, and it's bad," Milla says.

Yasaman's eyes grow round.

"Not about Max or Stewy!" Milla says. "About the Snack Attack, and Cheezy D'lites, and the company that's in charge of Cheezy D'lites."

"Happy Healthy Farms," Yasaman supplies.

"Right. And Happy Healthy Farms isn't a nice company. They make other stuff besides Cheezy D'lites, like frozen chicken nuggets, and also Munchy Lunchies."

"I brought a Munchy Lunchy today," Violet says. Munchy Lunchies are prepacked lunches, like for taking to school, and they usually include chips, fruit, a drink, and some sort of main thing, like mini-corndogs or do-it-yourself pizzas.

"What kind?" Milla asks.

"BLT," Violet says.

"Well, you're going to have to throw it away," Milla says. "Because what is bacon made of? Pigs. And guess what? The pigs they use are treated really badly. They're taken away from their moms when they're babies, and since they can't suck on their moms'"—she grimaces—"*you knows*, guess what happens?"

Violet looks alarmed. "What?"

"They suck each other's tails. The baby pigs are crammed all together in a pen, and they want to suck on something, so they suck each other's tails, but then they get infected, because they chew on them and stuff, too. So do you know what the Happy Healthy Farms people do?"

"I don't think I want to," Violet says.

"They *cut them off.*" Milla looks from face to face. "They just cut the baby pigs' tails off no matter what— and they don't use any kind of antiseptic. *Anesthetic.*" She groans and presses the palm of her heel to her forehead. "They don't use painkillers is what I'm saying. Isn't that awful?"

Violet looks ill. "Will someone share their lunch with me?"

Milla plows ahead. "And there's other stuff, too. Like, the chickens they use never get to see the sun, and they give them hormones to make them grow fast, only then they grow so fast that their legs break, because they can't hold up their own fat bodies."

"That's awful," Yasaman says.

"I know," Milla says. "So I totally agree with the Cheezy D'lite ban, because we shouldn't be buying stuff from Happy Healthy Farms, period. I think we need to get the whole grade in on it and do a protest or something. Maybe tomorrow, during assembly?"

The girls look at one another. Every Friday, both fifth-grade classes gather in the commons before morning

271

break. The teachers make anouncements, kids give presentations, sometimes Ms. Westerfeld brings in special guests. Stuff like that.

"I bet everyone would want to know how phony Happy Healthy Farms is," Violet says. "Not just us."

"We'd have to be polite, though," Yasaman says. "We couldn't march around or dye anyone orange."

Milla never imagined kids marching around dyeing one another orange. She was just thinking someone would make a speech, and then all the fifth graders could thrust their fists in the air and say, "End the suffering!" Or something like that.

"Um, agreed," she says.

"Let's do it," Violet says passionately. "Let's round everyone up and have a secret meeting."

Katie-Rose claps her hands, almost like a cheerleader. "Okay, then." She turns, opens her mouth wide, and yells, "Hey! People! Get over here!"

A few kids look over.

"Just the fifth graders," Katie-Rose commands. "And yes, Max, that includes you."

Milla's heart thumps. Max looks confused, but he

approaches with the other fifth graders. At first, Milla focuses on Max's shirt (blue plaid and painfully cute), but then Milla steels herself and lifts her head to meet his gaze.

He tries to smile. It's the most heartbreaking smile she's seen in her life.

Thirty

The fifth graders have all gathered in a clump on the field, surely not looking the *slightest* bit suspicious. Anyway, the teachers don't seem to care as long as no one starts fighting or yelling. Everyone's excited. Everyone's throwing out ideas for the Snack Attack. Becca wants to have a school dance, and the ticket money could go to animal rights. Olivia wants to make bumper stickers. Brannen wants to shoot off fireworks to spell a message, like "Save the Pigs! Down with Bacon!"

"Dude, no way," Chance says. "Bacon rocks."

"Even if it means hurting pigs?" Milla says. She's being surprisingly forward, challenging even the rowdy boys like Chance and Preston. The only boy Milla *isn't* interacting with is Max. Who isn't rowdy at all.

"There are farmers who raise pigs humanely," Milla says. "You don't have to give up bacon entirely. Just don't buy it from Happy Healthy Farms."

"How about 'Eat Lettuce'?" Olivia suggests. "For the firework message?"

"I love fireworkth," Natalia says. She makes eye contact with Yasaman. "Hi, Yathaman."

"Um, hi," Yasaman says. She checks to see where Katie-Rose is, her gut fluttering even though technically there's no reason for it to.

. Natalia smiles behind her headgear. "Thankth again for our talk yetherday."

"Uh-huh," Yasaman says. Other kids are throwing out Snack Attack ideas, so she says, "Let's listen, 'kay?"

"What talk?" Katie-Rose says, edging farther from Milla and Olivia and closer to Yasaman.

"It was nothing," Yasaman tells her.

Natalia makes an indignant sound. She steps closer

to Katie-Rose. "I wath the one who told Yathaman"—she lowers her voice—*"what Milla did."*

"You were?" Katie-Rose says. She turns to Yasaman. "She was?"

"Can we talk about this later?" Yasaman asks. She feels sickish. "I want to listen to people's ideas." She edges away, but not before overhearing Natalia's next proclamation.

"And Yathaman apologithed to me for how rude you've been. Tho I *gueth* I forgive you."

"Oh, you *do*, do you?" Katie-Rose says.

Yasaman blends deeper into the crowd. She pays desperate attention to Carmen, who's raising her hand even though they're not in class and no one's the teacher. She ignores the tingling of dread at the base of her spine, because what's said is said, right? It's not as if Yasaman was wrong to smooth things out with Natalia. It's *good* to smooth things out with people.

"Last year?" Carmen said. "On the Fourth of July? My little brother put a sparkler in his diaper."

"Dude, bad idea," Preston says, doubling over and actually putting his hands over his crotch. Yasaman looks *very* quickly away from that, and Quin, who notices, smirks.

"No fireworks," Violet says with authority. "Bumper stickers are fine for later, but we don't have time to do that before tomorrow. For tomorrow, we just need, like, a presentation."

"A polite presentation," Milla contributes.

"That tells everyone how we're not going to put up with it anymore," Violet says. "All the lying and unhealthiness and stuff."

"Yeah," Yasaman says.

"We should do the Chicken Dance!" Chance says. "Only we could make it the *Dead* Chicken Dance, and at the end we could die, like this!" He squawks and flaps his elbows and puts his hands around his throat. His squawks grow raspier and more tortured. He falls to the ground, and kids clap.

"Uh-huh, do that," Quin says sourly. Yasaman thinks again that it's interesting how with Modessa out of the picture, Quin actually *can* function, even if it's in an obnoxious, wanting-the-Snack-Attack-to-fail sort of way. But earlier this morning, Yasaman overheard Mr.

Emerson tell Ms. Perez he was going to call Modessa's parents, so she'll probably be back soon, unfortunately.

"No Chicken Dance," Violet says.

"Aw, come on," Preston protests. "The Dead Chicken Dance is a winner. It's got drama, suspense—"

"Poo," says Elena, who lives on a farm. Not a factory farm, but the good kind. "Chickens poo everywhere."

"Poo," Preston repeats, chortling.

That unleashes a flood of poo comments from everyone—"Poo is pooey." "There was poo in my brother's diaper. It got on the sparkler!" "Down with poo!"—and Yasaman starts giggling and can't stop. There's so much energy buzzing through the crowd, and it all has to do with the Snack Attack. Or at least most of it. She's ignoring Katie-Rose and Natalia, who might possibly be engaged in a heated exchange.

But still. How amazing that all of this force and motivation started out with *her*. It's incredible!

There's a flash of rainbow and the bounce of pompoms, and a scowling Katie-Rose appears by her side, sticking her face right up close to Yasaman's. That *scowl*—it makes Yasaman dry right up.

"Katie-Rose?" Yasaman says. Her heart whams, and she thinks *Natalia*, though she doesn't want to go there out loud.

"This is not the time or the place," Katie-Rose says in a low voice. "And I'm trying very hard to, like, be a better person. Because of Milla."

"That's . . . that's good."

"Very *very* hard." Katie-Rose lifts her chin. "But I want you to think about . . . things, and I want you to look into your heart and decide what being a good friend means. To Milla, but also to me. And that is all."

She turns to go, then turns right back. "Okay, actually it's not. You shouldn't be so impressed with Natalia's buttons, because guess what? Natalia totally stole the 'Why Snackrifice?' slogan. She said she made it up, but she didn't. It's on the Wheat Thins box! I saw it when I made Milla a snack yesterday!"

"She . . . what?"

"I was going to keep it to myself. So just ask yourself this, Yasaman. If Natalia lied about that, what else might she be lying about?" She gives Yasaman a hard stare. "And that really is all I have to say. So good-bye for real."

She spins on her heel and bumps into Chance, who flings his hands up and screams a high-pitched scream. Because Chance and Preston are still doing that, pretending to be scared whenever Katie-Rose gets too close.

Katie-Rose flushes and strides off. Yasaman is stunned. Around her, kids continue to make poo comments, while Violet tries to get them back on track.

Milla steps up next to Yasaman. "So what do you think?" she asks. "Should Elena bring her pig?"

"Um, I didn't know she was considering it."

Milla hip-bumps Yasaman. Her eyes are bright. Possibly *too* bright. "Haven't you been paying attention, goofball? Elena has a potbelly pig as a pet, and Elena says her dad could bring it tomorrow for the presentation. It weighs two hundred pounds!"

"Wow," Yasaman says.

"When we give our speech, Porkchop could just be up there with us. It would be like, 'See? Do you really want to eat *me*?!'"

"Its name's Porkchop?"

"He's very affectionate, Elena says," Milla goes on.

"Elena says pigs are very social. They need friends just like we do. Isn't that cool?"

It *is* cool, and yet it isn't, because sometimes a friend needing a friend doesn't equal a friend being a friend, or getting a friend, or something. That's what Yasaman thinks, and her body agrees.

"My stomach hurts," she says, giving Milla a troubled smile. "I'm going to ask if I can go to the bathroom. Thanks, though. For talking."

Yasaman crosses the playground, and the Snack Attack chaos grows fainter. She walks up to Ms. Perez and asks if she can go to the bathroom.

Mr. Emerson, who is standing by Ms. Perez, snaps his fingers. "Nutmeg!"

"Right!" Ms. Perez says.

Yasaman looks at them both, confused. "Nutmeg?"

"Sorry, Yasaman," Ms. Perez says. "And of course you can go to the bathroom. Just come back to class afterward, if morning break is over." She gives Mr. Emerson an amused smile. "You'll have to make me some, if your oven doesn't catch on fire again."

Mr. Emerson laughs, and despite her aching tummy, Yasaman notices that the two teachers seem to like each other. Like, really like each other, the way friends do or possibly even more.

But with the Snack Attack, plus Milla's bright eyes, plus Porkchop the two-hundred-pound pig, she has too many things to think about, especially with Katie-Rose's burning words hogging most of the space.

In the bathroom, she tries to process, again, the mess of herself, Katie-Rose, and Natalia.

She wishes she hadn't apologized to Natalia on Katie-Rose's behalf. She didn't mean to make Katie-Rose feel as if she'd gone behind her back.

She did, though, didn't she?

As for the "Why Snackrifice?" slogan, well, that's just weird. Natalia claimed she worked so hard on the slogan that she got a migraine. But if it came from a Wheat Thins box . . .

Why would Natalia lie about something so meaningless?

Yasaman leans forward, her elbows on her knees and her head in her hands.

Lying isn't okay. Meanness isn't okay. But hurting a friend's feelings isn't okay, either. Hurting even a non-friend's feelings isn't okay.

Which is more important: being a good friend or a good person?

Her mind goes to Nigar, and how Nigar's teacher said, "No more crying at drop-off." Yasaman's *ana* made a "Good Drop-off Chart" to help Nigar do better, with a box to fill in for each day of the school week. If Nigar doesn't cling to their *ana* and cry when it's time for her to leave, then Nigar gets to draw a smiley face in that day's box. If Nigar has five smiley faces at the end of the week, then their *ana* will take Nigar out for ice cream.

Not clinging to their *ana* is really hard for Nigar. But it's got to be hard for their *ana*, too. If Nigar was clinging to Yasaman and crying, "Don't go, don't go," could Yasaman pry Nigar off and walk away, even if she knew it was for Nigar's own good?

Oh, wow, Yasaman thinks, having an aha moment about Natalia and Nigar and even Katie-Rose. Especially Katie-Rose. The basic *aha* has to do with how life is hard for everyone. The specifics are more complex.

Last month, Katie-Rose got mad at Modessa for making "rules" about who Milla could talk to and who she couldn't. But isn't she doing the exact same thing to Yasaman now? Yes, she is.

But . . . Katie-Rose *isn't* Modessa. She's spazzy sometimes, and bossy, but deep down Yasaman knows Katie-Rose doesn't want to hurt anyone.

With Modessa, Katie-Rose was on the outside wanting in. Now Katie-Rose is the one on the inside. . . . Is it possible she's scared of losing that?

As for Natalia, Yasaman's *aha* is that Natalia is like a very large preschooler. Just as Nigar wants to cling to their *ana,* Natalia wants to cling to Yasaman. And—oh, wow, here comes another *aha,* this time about herself— Yasaman hasn't done much to discourage her.

Yasaman still thinks Katie-Rose is more in the wrong than she is, and she still feels bad for Natalia. Natalia just wants friends, that's all. Nonetheless, Yasaman is finally beginning to understand where Katie-Rose is coming from.

Thirty-one

Violet

The Snack Attack planning session is over. There will be no fireworks, but there will be a pig, as long as Elena's dad is available to bring it. Oh, and as long as Ms. Westerfeld gives her permission. In an amazing display of courage, Milla volunteered to go to Ms. Westerfeld and do the asking; that's where she is now.

As for Violet, she is glowing as she heads toward the building with the rest of her class. She's the one who kept everyone focused out on the field (as focused as a bunch of wild fifth graders could be), and she's the one who came up with the official lineup for tomorrow: speech (Katie-Rose), pig (Elena), and a *modified* version of the Dead Chicken Dance (Chance, Preston, Brannen). Then, on Violet's cue, all the fifth graders will cry out in unison, "Happy Healthy Farms hurt happy healthy animals!" And Yasaman will present Ms. Westerfeld with a signed petition begging Rivendell to stop supporting such an evil company.

Milla catches up with Violet and says, "That went well, don't you think? You're such a good leader. Like, a natural leader."

"Thanks," Violet says. She grabs Milla's forearm to slow her down, letting the other kids go ahead of them. "Hey, Mills . . . are you doing okay?"

Milla flashes a smile. Only, it's more just the shape of a smile. "Oh, you know." She changes the subject. "What about *you*? How was your visit with your mom?"

"It was good," Violet says.

"Yeah?" Milla says.

Violet pauses. Everyone else has gone inside. "Yeah," she says slowly. "I mean, it was weird, and the hospital smelled funny, but it wasn't as awful as I thought it would be."

"Oh, Violet, that's *great*," Milla says, and if her tone doesn't fully match up with her words, well, Violet doesn't hold it against her.

"See you at lunch?" Milla says. Milla has keyboarding next, while Violet has German. For those classes, which are called "specials," the fifth graders get mixed up so that everyone gets to know one another. That goes for art, music, PE, and Spanish, too.

Violet nods, and Milla gives her another smile. This one's more real, even if it's a sad-real. Then Milla pulls open the door and disappears into the building.

Violet follows, taking her time. As her eyes adjust from outside light to inside light, she hears someone clear his throat.

It's Cyril, standing to the side of the door. He seems to be waiting for her, but Violet has no idea why.

"Cyril?" she says.

Nothing.

"Did you want something?"

Still nothing, and Violet feels a trickle of sweat at the back of her neck. Did Cyril . . . omigosh, did he hear what she said to Milla?

"If you want something, you should say it, because otherwise I'm leaving."

His lips part, but he doesn't speak. She waits maybe two seconds, growing increasingly distressed, then fast-walks down the hall. She takes her seat in Mrs. Gundeck's room, but she can't stop thinking about him. He slinks in after her—he has German, too, because she's just that lucky—and the sight of him makes her body heat up.

In the front of the room, Mrs. Gundeck starts her lesson. Violet tries not to fidget, because Mrs. Gundeck is strict and threatens to duct tape kids to their desks if they don't stop wiggling and pay attention. Of course, this makes most kids wiggle even more, because it's so fun to see Mrs. Gundeck get worked up.

But Violet isn't that type of kid, and she isn't being disrespectful on purpose. She just can't get interested in the German words for various body parts. So *der Kopf* means "the head" and *der Fuß* means "the foot." How can she possibly care about that with Cyril swimming around in her brain?

His shirt today says "Employee of the Month," but Cyril doesn't have a job. He's ten, for heaven's sake.

Ag, Violet thinks. His crazy shirts. His crazy behavior. His dark eyes staring at her, his mouth opening and shutting.

And that *notebook*! He's writing in it again, right this second. He's writing whatever mysterious things he feels compelled to put down, and maybe he's writing about her or maybe not, but how can she know unless she sees for herself?

"Now, who can tell me the German word for 'arm'?" Mrs. Gundeck asks.

"No idea," Thomas says. "What's the German word for 'bottom'?"

"Inappropriate," Mrs. Gundeck says as the class titters.

"Whoa, that is just weird," Thomas says. He turns to Max. "Sit on your *inappropriate*, young man."

The laughter builds, and if not for Cyril, Violet would probably join in.

"Thomas, I will spank your *Hintern* if you don't behave," Mrs. Gundeck threatens. She never would really, but she's always saying she will. Plus, she's German. In Germany, she has told the class, students get spanked all the time.

"She's going to spank my *inappropriate!*" Thomas says in a stage whisper. "Oh no!"

Thomas is being funny, and Violet knows he's doing it to cheer Max up, which is sweet. But she can't stop brooding about Cyril. She came to school feeling better about her mom than she's felt in a long time—and now here Cyril is, triggering her anxiety all over again. She has to find out what he knows about her mom, and the only way to do that is to get her hands on his notebook. *It's the only way.*

She'll find out once and for all what he knows, and then . . . and then she'll deal with it. She'll finally be able to move on.

She glances over her shoulder and sees that Cyril isn't paying attention to Thomas's antics, either. He's hunched over his *notebook*, his *evil* notebook, and if he hooked his pinkie into the corner of his mouth and smiled deviously, he would be the spitting image of Dr. Evil himself.

Violet feels the hot pressure of tears, because *it's not fair.* When she feels good, everything seems doable, and she's able to focus on what's important. Like Milla. Like the Snack Attack. But when she feels bad, everything falls apart.

It's as if the words scrawled in Cyril's notebook are connected to one end of a piece of thread, and Violet is connected to the other. When he writes, he's tugging on Violet's end of the thread, and Violet is unraveling.

"What about teeth?" Thomas calls out. "How do you say 'teeth' in German?"

"*Zzzzt,*" Mrs. Gundeck says sharply, because the class is unraveling, too. They know Thomas doesn't care what the German word for "teeth" is, and they're excited to see where he's going with this. Becca bounces in her seat, so ready to laugh that her mouth has fallen wide open.

"Becca, close your mouth. I can see your tonsils," Mrs. Gundeck says.

"No, you can't," Becca replies giddily. "I don't *have* tonsils!"

"It's true!" Carmen says. "She got them taken out when she was seven!"

"Class," Mrs. Gundeck says. She claps the preschool clap: *clap-clap-clapclapclap.* No one echoes the pattern back to her, because *ha ha,* they're having too much fun being wild.

Violet rises from her desk, her *inappropriate* hovering over her seat. When Mrs. Gundeck isn't looking, Violet slides in a crouched position into the aisle.

The kids near her notice, but Violet can't worry about them. She can't worry about Carmen, who gapes at her as she sidles past, and she can't worry about Preston, except to stomp on his toe when he opens his mouth as if to ask what the heck she's doing, creeping to the back of the room like a spy.

"But, Mrs. Gundeck, the reason I want to know the German word for 'teeth' is because I have something to say about teeth," Thomas explains.

"No," Mrs. Gundeck says.

"About *your* teeth, Mrs. Gundeck!" Thomas presses. He stands up from his desk, which is a blessing, because it distracts the kids from Violet. "And it's a good thing, I promise."

"Sit *down*, Thomas," Mrs. Gundeck says.

Violet is within touching distance of Cyril, who is so focused on what he's writing that he doesn't notice. She could grab his notebook right now, but she tells her itchy fingers to wait. *Let Thomas finish his joke about teeth,* she says silently. *And when everyone laughs . . .*

"Please, Mrs. G?" Thomas says.

"Fine," Mrs. Gundeck says, giving up. "Go ahead, Thomas."

He places his hand over his heart. "Mrs. G, your teeth are like the moon."

"Awww," Preston says. Tonsil-free Becca can't stop laughing. Violet snakes her hand toward Cyril's notebook. *Closer . . . closer . . .*

"Do you want to know why?" Thomas asks.

"I do not," Mrs. Gundeck says.

"Because they only come out at night!" Thomas says. "Just like the moon!"

Max moans and puts his head in his hands.

Becca says, "Huh?"

"Like a vampire! Get it?"

"No," Becca says.

"You mean a *werewolf*," Max says. "A *werewolf's* teeth only come out at night. You showed me that joke in your joke book."

"A werewolf," Mrs. Gundeck repeats. "Thomas? Did you just call me a werewolf?"

"Aw, Mrs. G, you know I was just—"

Mrs. Gundeck bares her teeth and growls, and people scream, especially Thomas, because it's freaky when a crotchety old German teacher turns one of her student's jokes back on the student himself. Mrs. Gundeck belly-laughs, and the class joins in, loud and out of control and still recovering from the shock.

This is Violet's chance, and she takes it. She snatches Cyril's notebook, and his pen scars the paper, leaving a painful blue gash.

"Hey!" he yelps, but everyone is laughing at Thomas and Mrs. Gundeck, and no one pays attention to Cyril, anyway, which gives Violet a pang. Her eyes go to him, full of remorse even though she had to do it. But *his* eyes, they're ...

Not something Violet can look at right now.

And she's not giving back the notebook, not until after she's read it. And anyway, Cyril won't cry, because Cyril can't cry. Cyril is incapable of crying.

"What did you do?" Carmen asks as Violet slides back into her desk. She glances at what Violet's got. "Is that Cyril's notebook? Did you steal Cyril's notebook?!"

"Don't be ridiculous," Violet says, her voice catching. "I told him I'd proofread a story he wrote. Now, shush." She's shaking with adrenaline, and with other things, too, like the image of Cyril's eyes, and the emotions she saw there, which she assumed he didn't feel.

With trembling hands, she opens his notebook, because she has to. Cyril's writing is cramped and small, but surprisingly neat. Block letters. Dark, like he presses down hard on the pencil.

"All right, class, we've had our fun," Mrs. Gundeck says. "Back to work, or I will bite you all." She passes out a "Body Parts" worksheet, and as the others chatter quietly and fill out the answers, Violet looks through Cyril's notebook for answers of her own.

She starts at the beginning, skimming for mentions of her or her mother. Anything. It's tricky to decipher, though. It's written in some sort of code.

Aug. 22: nothing

Aug. 23: nothing

All through August, the entries say "nothing," with one exception.

Aug. 29: Mr. E: "Nice shirt, Cyril." And after the words, a star: ☆

Oh no, she thinks. She skims for other entries with stars and finds one a few pages later.

Sept. 4: Pam: "Would you like chocolate milk or white?" ☆

In addition to her front-desk duties, Pam is the lunch lady. Usually, when kids go through the lunch line, they grab their own milk, but on this day maybe Cyril forgot, and so Pam had to ask?

A blanket of fear drops over her heart, but Violet keeps reading.

Sept. 12: Ms. W: "Cyril, how's your stomach? Your

mom told me you're trying some new strategies.
Would you like to talk about how it's going? Yes?
No? Okay, Cyril. Well, I'm always here. You know
that. And if it gets too bad, you know you can
come to the office and rest on the mat."

No stars for that one, Violet notes. Maybe because Ms. Westerfeld is the principal. Maybe because principals are just too . . . principal-y sometimes.

And then comes a big entry. Violet gets a sour taste in her mouth.

Sept. 19: M: "The next one's worth fifty points.
But you have to touch his head."
Q: "Ew! That's worth a hundred points at least."
M: "Fine, a hundred points. If you bring back
a hair."
Q: "Ewwww! No way am I touching his greasy
hair!"

Violet knows what's coming next. She does. She does not know, however, that the "V," which stands for Violet, will be decorated. With wings. The "V" has wings.

V: "That's right, you're not. Why can't you
just leave him alone?" ☆☆☆☆☆

It goes on. The fight with Modessa and Quin, and Violet telling them how uncalled for their behavior is (did she really say that? uncalled for?), and finally ending with this, which Quin said after Violet grabbed her wrist to stop her from poking Cyril again:

Q: "What's your problem? Let go!"

V: "Not until you stop." ✰✰✰✰✰✰✰

Oh oh oh, Violet thinks. She stole Cyril's notebook . . . and his eyes, when she snatched it . . . and all this time, what he's been writing hasn't been mean at all. It's been . . . starry. Golden. Winged.

Finish, she tells herself. The day in the office, when he was on the mat. What did he write about her on the day in the office?

Her breath is shallow as she reads the entry:

Sept. 20: McGreevy: "Ah, Cyril-of-the-tumultuous-tummy. What you need are some digestive biscuits, you know. My mum? Best digestive biscuits ever. Swears by them. And tea! Nothing a spot of tea can't fix, am I right? Well. Yes. Never have been the talkative type, have you? Nothing wrong with that. Nothing a spot of tea can't—Oh, right. I already said that, didn't I? Well, let's get your mat out, then, shall we? That's a good lad. You are a good lad, Cyril. The other blokes, you can't let them—Yes. The mat. Never could shut my trap, says my mum. Guess that makes us perfect company, eh, mate?"

There are three stars after that entry. ☆☆☆ Then there's more, like Ms. Westerfeld checking on him, and Preston walking by and making a mean joke about Cyril being a preschool baby on a preschool baby mat. And Violet, the whole time she's reading, she thinks, *I didn't know. I didn't know, I didn't know.*

At the bottom of the page, Violet appears. Again, there are wings on the "V," but they're no longer blazing and strong. This time they're folded in.

The words next to her name are "I miss you, too, Mom."

She closes the notebook, her vision blurry. She stands, walks to Cyril's desk, and holds out his notebook.

Cyril doesn't take it.

"Here," she whispers. "I'm . . . sorry."

"Violet?" Mrs. Gundeck says. "Is there a problem?"

Before she can answer, Cyril grabs his notebook. Then he yanks the cover off and tears the pages out, shredding them into bits. His breathing is labored and his face is red.

Thomas says, "Dude."

Becca laughs nervously.

"Cyril?" Mrs. Gundeck says.

"Cyril?" Violet echoes. "Will you just ... will you please just look at me?"

He won't. He rips and shreds and crumples.

The whole room grows silent, except for the ocean roaring in Violet's head. Cyril is no longer swimming in it, because he's no longer swimming, period. He's floundering, thrashing, gasping.

Drowning.

Thirty-two

Camilla

Milla is in the computer lab, helping a monkey climb from tree to tree to get bananas. Well, she's supposed to be, but her monkey has gotten no farther than the first tree.

Ms. Westerfeld said yes to the "nutrition presentation" Milla proposed, and after hearing for herself how passionate Milla was, she suggested inviting the younger grades and the preschoolers to come listen, too. Milla was temporarily elated, but once she got to keyboarding class, her elation evaporated like steam.

The game she's supposed to be playing has a sound track of jazzy jungle drums. The monkey is cute and rascally, and if Milla types the letter *U* like she's supposed to, he hops from one tree to a higher tree. And there are bananas on that higher-up tree! Yum!

But instead of typing *U*, she types *M*, and a coconut plummets from above. It knocks the monkey from the tree, and he screeches when he hits the ground.

Ms. Karbula, the keyboarding teacher, is helping Carmen place her hands in the right position, and Milla knows she'll be busy for a while. Carmen can't for the life of her come to grips with putting her pinkie on the semicolon key.

Milla navigates away from Keyboard Climber and goes to LuvYaBunches.com. She'll make another stab at a blog entry, she decides. Because all these sad feelings . . . she has to let them out somehow, and talking to a computer is better than talking to no one.

Words appear on the screen: **Post an entry?**

Milla takes a deep breath, lets it out, and starts typing.

I am being sad and depressive today.

I think Max is, too.

He was nice to me on the playground, but that's just cuz that's the way he is. I'm glad he doesn't hate me, tho. Thx for telling me that, Katie-Rose. But even if he doesn't hate me, I know he doesn't *like* me anymore. Not like he used to.

nvm, this is a stupid entry. I'm going to delete it anyway.

I just wanted to say I'm sorry.

Stewy? I'm really sorry.

Milla looks at the words on the screen. She uses Select All to highlight the entire entry and hits Delete.

Thirty-three

Yasaman

After school lets out, Yasaman waits in Ms. Perez's room while everyone else—including Katie-Rose, who glares at the ground rather than look at her, and including Chance, who succeeds in tripping Katie-Rose since Katie-Rose isn't watching where she's going—files out.

"Yasaman?" Ms. Perez says when Yasaman is the only student left sitting at her desk.

Yasaman waves, which is kind of goofy. She shoves her hands under her thighs.

"Can I help you with something, sweetie?" Ms. Perez

says. She comes over and perches on Yasaman's desk. "What's up?"

"Um . . ." Now that she's here, alone, with her teacher, it's as if there's glue in her mind, which keeps her thoughts from coming out.

"Start with something easy," Ms. Perez suggests kindly.

"I . . ." she begins. She remembers what she overheard Ms. Perez say on the playground, when Ms. Perez was chatting with Mr. Emerson and Yasaman went over to ask if she could go to the bathroom. Something about nutmeg and—unless she totally misunderstood—Mr. Emerson's oven catching on fire?

"Did Mr. Emerson's *oven* catch on fire?" she asks.

Ms. Perez laughs. "Oh my word, can you believe it? He left a potholder in it, apparently."

"Why?"

"He was baking miniature pumpkin bread loaves to bring to the teachers' lounge. They didn't quite turn out, apparently." She smiles. "John dubbed them 'pumpkin bread–shaped disasters.'"

John, Yasaman thinks. *John Emerson.* "That's funny," she says. "Well, kind of funny and kind of sad."

305

"True," Ms. Perez says philosophically. "Life is like that, isn't it?"

"But why?" Yasaman asks. In a smushed-together rush, she adds, "I'm-not-talking-about-snacks."

"Hmm," Ms. Perez says. "What *are* you talking about? If you don't mind me asking."

"Well, like you said. Just life, and friends, and how sometimes everything starts off happy and then turns sad."

Ms. Perez looks concerned, but not too concerned. Just the right amount of concerned to hopefully give good advice without making Yasaman start to cry.

"Are you and Katie-Rose having problems?" she asks.

Yasaman nods.

"Is Natalia part of the mix, too?"

Yasaman nods again. She's surprised Ms. Perez knows, but then, there was the whole blowup when Katie-Rose got sent to the hall. So never mind. She's not surprised anymore.

"Poor Katie-Rose," Ms. Perez says. "And Chance and Preston aren't making things any easier for her, are they?" She sighs. "Then again, *she* isn't making things easy for herself, either."

"It's not her fault Chance and Preston are being mean to her," Yasaman says loyally. "I hate it when people are mean."

"I do, too," Ms. Perez says. She tilts her head. "You're a very nice person, Yasaman. You're also a rule follower, aren't you?"

What a strange thing to say. "Is that bad?"

"Not at all. It can make life hard, though." She smiles ruefully. "Harder than it already is."

Even stranger, Yasaman thinks. Don't teachers want kids to be nice rule-followers?

"I try to be nice myself," Ms. Perez says.

"You *are* nice."

"I'm also a rule follower, believe it or not."

"But you wear checkered stockings," Yasaman says without thinking.

Ms. Perez laughs. Yasaman's cheeks heat up.

"Small rebellions," Ms. Perez says. "Sometimes, Yasaman, you need to figure out how to follow the rules *and* follow your heart, even when it comes to checkered stockings. And I think—and this is just me, now—but I think it applies to friends, too."

Yasaman isn't sure exactly what Ms. Perez means, but she thinks she understands the underlying feeling of it. Like, that maybe a person doesn't have to be nice to everyone all the time. Or, maybe not that—nice *is* important—but maybe, in terms of friends, that you don't have to be friends with someone to the same degree that they want you to be? Like, you can be one girl's FFF and another girl's "hi at school" friend, even if the "hi at school" friend wants more?

Ms. Perez runs the back of her hand lightly over Yasaman's *hijab*. It's the equivalent of tousling the hair of a non-*hijab*–wearing girl, Yasaman figures. It makes her feel warm inside.

"I guess what I'm saying is that what you think you're supposed to do doesn't always match up with what you want to do. Sometimes you have to do what your *heart* tells you to do."

"Well, what I want is for Katie-Rose to like me again,"

she says slowly, hoping Ms. Perez won't laugh or react in some other way that makes Yasaman feel foolish.

"Yasaman," Ms. Perez says firmly. "I know without a doubt that Katie-Rose likes you." She pauses. "Is it possible that she thinks *you* no longer like *her*?"

"No," Yasaman responds on autopilot.

Ms. Perez lifts her eyebrows.

"If she did think that, she'd be wrong."

Ms. Perez laughs. "Well, people are wrong sometimes. People are wrong lots of the time. Anyway, liking people is easy. Trusting that they like you back is often harder."

"So what do I do?" Yasaman asks.

Ms. Perez uncrosses her legs and hops off Yasaman's desk. "Show her. Actions speak louder than words, you know."

"But how?"

Ms. Perez raps Yasaman's head. "That, sweet Yasaman, is up to you."

Friday, September 23

Thirty-four

Yasaman

aσaman is giddy on the way to school the
next morning. Because of the Snack Attack
presentation, scheduled to happen before morning
break, and also because of the perfume attack, unknown
to everyone except Yasaman, and scheduled to happen
whenever Yasaman decides the time is right.

Everyone knows about the Snack Attack, but the
perfume attack is her top secret plan to show Katie-Rose
she likes her. She came up with it last night, thanks to
Nigar, who used way too much body spray after her bath
and turned herself into a walking stink bomb.

Nigar is clearly perfume-obsessed (it was just last Sunday when she spilled their *ana*'s perfume everywhere!), and one day soon, Yasaman will need to sit Nigar down and give her a sister-to-sister talk about how "just a dab'll do it."

But last night, Nigar's smelliness was just the inspiration Yasaman needed.

Point one: Boys hate perfume. Yasaman could recall her *baba*'s scrunched up face when he came into the house last Sunday, and the memory made her giggle.

Point two: Perfume is supposed to smell like flowers, although it doesn't always, and sometimes it *is* too strong, like for example the Enchanted Orchid body spray her *büyükanne* gave her after hearing the story of the spilt-perfume disaster. The Blushing Cherry Blossom body spray she gave Nigar is slightly better, but still strong. Yasaman's *baba* said the girls were too young for perfume, but her *büyükanne* pooh-poohed him and said this way no more accidents would happen, since the Bath & Body Works body sprays came packaged in sturdy plastic bottles with spritzer nozzles.

Point three: Plastic perfume bottles with spritzer

nozzles are the perfect revenge for Chance and Preston. They'll be defeated with the fragrance of flowers—*ha ha ha ha ha ha!*

She pats the zippered pouch of her backpack, reassuring herself that both bottles of body spray are still there.

Her *ana* pulls into Rivendell's parking lot and parks. She twists to look at Nigar, who has yet to unbuckle herself, and says, "Remember, today is the day you get your treat. If this morning is a good drop-off—and I know it will be—you'll have filled out your entire chart!"

Nigar nods, clutching her Hello Kitty lunchbox. "Yes, because I am very proud of me."

"I am very proud of you, too," Yasaman says, patting Nigar's chubby leg.

"As am I," their *ana* says. "And do you remember what your treat is?"

"Tell me, tell me, tell me!"

"To drive to the ice-cream store and get ice creams! Won't that be fun?"

Yasaman expects Nigar to say "Yay!" Instead, her sister's face falls, and Yasaman feels a stab of alarm.

Everything is supposed to go right this morning. That will be a sign that everything is going to go right for the whole day.

"Küçüğüm!" their *ana* says. "Don't you want to go get ice creams?"

"Yes, but, *Ana,* I don't know how to drive!"

Yasaman laughs along with their *ana.*

"I will do the driving, Nigar," their *ana* says. "Your job is only to eat the ice cream."

"Oh," Nigar says. She looks at Yasaman and their *ana,* and since they're laughing, she does, too. "But *one day* I will drive, and if my little girl has good drop-offs, I will take *her* for ice cream."

She unfastens her seat belt and wiggles off of her booster. "And when I do, you can come, too, *Ana.*" She leans forward and taps Yasaman. "And you, because you are my bestest Yasaman."

Yasaman smiles. It *is* going to be a good day. She just knows it.

Thirty-five

Violet

Violet likes looking at the stars, and last night she tilted her blinds so that she could see them from her bed. She gazed at them and gazed at them until she fell asleep without even realizing it, which is the best way to do it. Then, when you wake up, you don't know what's real and what was a dream. You kind of do, but not for sure.

Violet *thinks* she dreamed that she, her mom, and Cyril all had tea together at a fancy restaurant. Only they didn't have tea; they had hot chocolate. The roof of the restaurant was made of glass, and they could see the stars above them, and the stars looked like mini-marshmallows.

She woke up feeling as if she'd had a good cry: wiped out, but also wiped clean. Ready for a fresh start.

So, dressed for success in a flippy black skirt, purple argyle vest, and purple flats, she gets to school early and waits for Cyril to arrive. She stands guard next to the office, because she knows Cyril will have to pass her in order to get to Mr. Emerson's room. Her heart is drumming in her chest, but so what? She folds her arms over her ribs and holds herself tight.

You can do this, she tells herself.

Yasaman arrives, accompanied by her mom and little sister. Yasaman darts over and says, "What's going on?"

"Nothing," Violet says. "Everything." She wavers, wondering if maybe she should just head to the fifth-grade classrooms with Yasaman. "I don't know."

Yasaman studies her, and then makes the most unexpected remark. "You're a very nice person, Violet."

"Ha," Violet retorts.

Yasaman squeezes her arm. "Find me before the

Snack Attack, all right? It's going to be awesome." Then she jogs off to catch up with her mom and sister.

Next through the door is a gaggle of second-grade girls talking about which Disney princess they may or may not be for Halloween, which is still a month away. The second graders are followed by Max, and he and Violet exchange hellos. After Max comes—

Whoa.

It's Modessa, back from the dead. She's flanked by her parents, and no one looks happy.

"Let's get this over with," Modessa's mother says, prodding Modessa to the front desk.

"But, Mo-o-m," Modessa whines.

"Shut it," Modessa's father says. "School is your job. Being an attorney is my job. And in order for *me* to get back to my job, *you* have to do your job. Nod if you understand."

Violet lifts one eyebrow. Who wants a father who says "shut it" and "nod if you understand"?

Sulking, Modessa nods.

"Then let's find this boy you have to apologize to," he says.

Well, Violet has no choice but to stay and watch now. *Poor Cyril,* she thinks. She spots him trudging through the door with a herd of kids, and she has the urge to run and shield him from the evil Medusa monster. She doesn't, of course.

"That's him," Modessa mutters, jerking her chin at Cyril. Cyril sees her and stops. He looks as strange and disheveled as ever. A boy knocks into him from behind, and he lurches forward.

Modessa's father exhales impatiently. He's wearing a suit, an expensive red tie, and an expression that suggests Cyril is hardly worth missing work for.

"Go on, then," he says. "Or wait. Do you have to have a witness?" He scans the entryway. His eyes land on Violet.

Oh, this is not good, she thinks.

"You," he says. "Come over here, please."

He says "please," but he doesn't mean it, she thinks. *He's just accustomed to being obeyed.* And Violet does obey him—or at least, her feet do, propelling her forward despite her reluctance to be part of what's to come.

"You, too," Modessa's father says to Cyril.

Cyril is frozen.

"Now," Modessa's father commands.

Where is Ms. Westerfeld? Violet wonders. *Where is Mr. McGreevy, or Pam the lunch lady, or any nice and normal adult whose presence would force Modessa's father to behave?*

But the commons is bustling with kids and chaos, and no one is there to save Cyril except Violet. And what can Violet possibly do?

Well, you did *get the most gold stars,* a rebel voice says inside her.

Stars! Like in her dream?

Mr. McGreevy came in at second place with three gold stars. But Violet got fifteen, if she counts every single one Cyril gave her.

(In his notebook, which she stole, and which he ripped to shreds when she returned it, pieces of paper fluttering to the ground like falling stars.)

Oh, whatever, she says to herself. *Don't worry about being a star. Just be real.*

"Hi, Cyril," she says, going to stand beside him. She looks directly at Modessa. "Hi, Modessa."

Modessa twists her face.

"Go on. Say what you need to say," Modessa's father says.

It's not about saying it. It's about meaning it, Violet thinks. She moves her body so that her arm is barely grazing Cyril's. Just a bit of human connection to say, *You're weird, but I am, too, and so are lots of people.*

His body relaxes a fraction of a degree.

"I'm sorry for how I behaved on the playground," Modessa recites, rolling her eyes.

"Great," Modessa's father says. "Done." He pins Violet with his lawyer's stare. "You. You'll tell whomever needs telling that Modessa has paid her debt to society?"

Violet nods curtly. She doesn't give him the ha-ha-yes-it's-stupid smile he seems to expect, and surprise flickers across his face. He seems—just for a moment—to actually *see* her. And then it's gone.

"Great," he says. "Then I suggest you all go to class."

Modessa stalks off. Violet doesn't have to obey Modessa's father any longer, however, so she stays put. So does Cyril. Their arms are still touching. Not in a bad way. Kids enter the building and move past them in a steady stream, and one of them is Milla, her eyebrows forming surprised peaks as she's swept along.

Violet? she seems to say.

Violet starts to reassure her, but she's distracted by the sight of Max, who hasn't yet gone to class, and who's gazing at Milla in the same worried way that Milla is gazing at her.

As Violet takes this in, the oddest sensation of clarity comes over her. Love is bigger than hurt. Love matters more than hurt. It doesn't have to be lovey-dovey love, either. It applies to all love.

Violet will go to Milla in a moment, and she'll tell her that bad things do happen. Mothers get sick. Hamsters die. People act stupid again and again and again. She'll tell Milla how all of this can be true, while at the same time, other truths can exist right alongside them. Like how she's pretty sure Max does still like Milla—like, *likes* her likes her—and how Milla is allowed to be happy about that, despite the sad stuff.

And how Yasaman is right that the Snack Attack is going to rock.

For now, she turns to Cyril, and she sees that his eyes aren't blank, bottomless pits after all. There are flecks of gold in his dark irises.

They don't say anything to each other . . . and yet, they kinda do. Not with words. Just with, like, a feeling that passes between them. But if they did speak, their exchange might sound like this:

Violet: I'm sorry about your notebook.

Cyril: Yeah. Well.

(beat)

Cyril: Um, thanks. About Modessa.

Violet: Yeah. Well.

(beat)

Violet: It was my pleasure. Really.

A grin comes and goes so quickly on Cyril's face that Violet can't be positive she saw it. Watching him move through the crowd, she wonders why in the world she ever found him spooky.

Thirty-six

Katie-Rose

Oh good golly, I should have given someone my video camera, Katie-Rose thinks at ten o'clock. The commons is filling up with kids, and Katie-Rose feels a surprising flutter of anxiety. *Why in the world didn't I give someone my video camera so they could record my speech?*

Well, too late now. *Too late, too late, too late*—and where are Milla and Yasaman and Violet? And Elena, and Porkchop the pig?

Milla hugs her from behind, draping herself over Katie-Rose's shoulders. "Ready, Freddy?"

"No, and don't call me Freddy," Katie-Rose says. Milla's

cheer seems slightly forced, and Katie-Rose suspects that while Milla does care about the Snack Attack, it's more like distraction therapy than anything else. And maybe a way to right a wrong, not that their presentation will bring Stewy back. But for Milla, it's not really about Healthy Happy Farms. It's about Stewy. It's about Max.

Katie-Rose gets that.

"Thanks for doing this," Milla says. "Because … well … it means a lot to me, that's all."

"I know," Katie-Rose says.

"No, really," Milla insists.

Katie-Rose holds her gaze. "No, really. I know."

Violet joins Milla and Katie-Rose. She scans the room, which is already crowded. The older kids are sitting in the back, and the preschoolers are sitting on the floor in the front. Chance and Preston are by the water fountain, practicing their Chicken Dance, and the rest of the fifth graders are standing in a block of solidarity at the far end of the room.

Violet whistles. "Holy mackerel. That's a lot of people."

Katie-Rose smiles tightly. She clutches her type-written speech, even though she's got it memorized.

Ms. Westerfeld approaches the three flower friends. "It's time to start, girls." She furrows her brow. "Where's Yasaman? Milla, didn't you tell me that Yasaman was part of this?"

Only the biggest part of all, Katie-Rose thinks, and then wishes she hadn't, because thinking about Yasaman is so painful. But you can't take back a thought, and anyway, it's true: Yasaman is the brainchild behind the Snack Attack. Even if Yasaman doesn't like Katie-Rose anymore, Katie-Rose is going to give the best possible speech she can.

Milla bites her lip. "Um, I'm sure she's here. Maybe she's—"

"There," Violet says, pointing at Rivendell's front door. She grins and says, *"Yes,"* because next to Yasaman is Elena, and next to Elena, on a leash, is the largest, most glorious pig Violet has ever seen.

"Porkchop," Katie-Rose marvels.

"Oh my word," Ms. Westerfeld mutters. But she agreed to this, so too bad for her if she's having second thoughts.

Kids squeal as Yasaman and Elena walk with

Porkchop to the front of the commons. Yasaman's eyes are huge, but she's beaming. A man with broad shoulders and a ponytail follows them, and Katie-Rose assumes he's Elena's dad.

"Try to keep it down, guys," he tells the Rivendell students. "We don't want to get Porkchop too excited."

If Porkchop *is* excited, he's hiding it well. He lumbers along beside Elena, snuffling occasionally and placidly taking in the scene.

"That is one massive pig," Preston says, moving closer.

"I know," Katie-Rose says.

"Hope he doesn't get scared when he looks at you," Chance says, and Katie-Rose glowers.

"All right," Ms. Westerfeld says, as if coming out of a trance. She steps to the front of the room and tries to get everyone's attention. It takes a l-o-n-g time, as Porkchop has stolen the show, and the show hasn't even started.

"If you want to stay, you will put your hands in your laps and be quiet," Ms. Westerfeld finally says. "Otherwise, I'm sure your teachers would be happy to take you back to your classrooms."

Everyone hushes immediately. Nigar, in the front row,

waves at Katie-Rose, and Katie-Rose waves back. Then she realizes Nigar was probably waving at Yasaman, or possibly Porkchop. Along with Elena, they've taken their places at the front of the room.

"Sit," Elena tells Porkchop, and Porkchop sits. Everyone murmurs with glee.

"You're on," Ms. Westerfeld says.

"Knock 'em dead," Yasaman whispers.

Katie-Rose looks at Yasaman in surprise, and Yasaman gives her a thumbs-up. *Wow*, Katie-Rose thinks. She feels a thousand times bigger all of a sudden. As big as Porkchop.

She steps forward. "Um, hi," she says to the entire student body. "I'm Katie-Rose, and this is Porkchop. Porkchop the pig. Porkchop belongs to Elena"—Elena waves—"and he's here because . . ." She falters. "Because . . ." Her mouth is dry, and her words have all gone away.

Modessa titters from the sidelines. Of course, today is the day she decided to come back.

"Because he's your best friend?" she says, making some of the kids laugh.

"*No*," Katie-Rose says.

"Ignore her," Violet says dangerously.

"Because of the *Snack Attack*," Yasaman prompts in a whisper.

The Snack Attack! Right! Katie-Rose stands up straight and tall and clasps her hands behind her, military style.

"Porkchop is here because pigs are very educational," she says, giving a nod to Ms. Westerfeld, "and also because we, the fifth graders, would like to tell you some very important things that you should know."

She doesn't look at Ms. Westerfeld anymore, because she suspects that Milla might not have told Ms. Westerfeld every last detail of what Katie-Rose plans to cover. Especially since, um, Katie-Rose might not have told *Milla* every last detail of what she plans to cover.

"Porkchop leads a happy life," Katie-Rose tells the audience. "On sunny days, he gets to feel the warm rays of sunshine on his back, and when it rains, he gets to go inside." She looks at Elena, and Elena nods.

"But billions of other pigs—and also chickens and cows—aren't as lucky as Porkchop, because their owners aren't as nice as Elena and her dad. Did you know that in factory farms, little baby piggies are crammed so close together that they can't even turn around? And so they bite each other's tails off?"

Milla makes a small sound as if to correct her, but Katie-Rose plows on. She can see Ms. Westerfeld out of the corner of her eye, and she seems to be frowning, and Katie-Rose doesn't want to give her the opportunity to jump in.

"And do you know how they kill the pigs, when it's time to turn them into bacon?"

"Pigs get turned into bacon?" a preschooler asks. His eyes grow round. "Will Porkchop be turned into bacon?"

"Katie-Rose," Ms. Westerfeld warns.

"No, of course not," Katie-Rose says quickly. "But other pigs, in the *not* nice farms, sometimes they're bonked on their heads or thrown onto the cement floor. The meanies who work there just grab them by their feet and slam them down! *Bam!*"

Two preschoolers start to cry.

"Why?" asks a stricken second grader.

"So that *you* can have your yummy bacon for breakfast," Katie-Rose says. The second grader starts to cry, and Katie-Rose tries to soften the blow. "Not *just*

you, but everyone who's ever eaten bacon. And by the way, the same goes for chickens and cows, about being bonked and stuff."

"Katie-Rose, that's enough," Ms. Westerfeld says, stepping forward.

"What about sausage McGriddles?" a boy asks. "I had a sausage McGriddle this morning."

Katie-Rose sidles away from Ms. Westerfeld as she says, "Well, that delicious sausage McGriddle you ate— and they *are* delicious; believe me, I know—could have been our friend Porkchop here."

Elena's dad snorts, which throws Katie-Rose off, as does the sight of Ms. Westerfeld coming at her with grim determination. Also, the preschool teachers are trying to round up their charges and leave before the presentation is even over—rude!—but the sudden mass of squirmy three- and four-year-olds pens in Ms. Westerfeld.

Katie-Rose speaks quickly, knowing she's living on borrowed time. "And you guys know where chicken nuggets come from, right? Like the kind in Munchy Lunchies?"

Kids exchange looks of dread. Katie-Rose is betting

there will be lots of hungry Rivendell students at the end of the school day.

"They come from *murdered chickens*. And would you like to know how those murdered chickens meet their terrible fates?"

"No, Katie-Rose, they would *not*," Ms. Westerfeld says. She's almost to her, while Ms. Perez is closing the gap from the opposite side.

"Yes, we do!" a fourth grader wearing glasses calls out.

"Unless they get banged on their heads, too," a girl says. "Please tell me they're not banged on their heads. *Please.*"

Other girls make praying hands and add their "pleases" to the fray. The noise brings Porkchop to his feet. He grunts, and some of the first and second graders go *eeek!* and scoot backward into their neighbors.

"*Sit,*" Elena tells Porkchop, but Porkchop doesn't.

"It's okay, buddy," Elena's dad says. He's leaning against the wall by the water fountain. To the packed room of kids, he says, "He gets excited if there's too much noise, but Porkchop's not going to hurt you. Still, I reckon it's about time to wrap this up, huh?"

"No!" lots of kids complain.

"Yes," Ms. Westerfeld says, angling sideways to avoid a stray preschooler.

"But we haven't heard about the murdered chickens!" says the boy wearing glasses.

"Well—" Katie-Rose says, but she's knocked back by Chance, Preston, and Brannen. They take over the show, flapping their wings and shaking their tailfeathers as they belt out the lyrics to the Chicken Dance.

"I don't wanna be a chicken, I don't wanna be a duck, so I shake my butt, nah nah nah nah!"

Porkchop grunts. He dips his head low, then raises it sharply up, throwing Elena off balance. Elena's father snaps into action, pushing off the wall and rapidly closing the distance between himself and his daughter.

"Sit, Porkchop!" Elena says.

"Boys, stop!" Ms. Westerfeld commands.

Instead, the boys move straight into the neck-strangling, coughing, falling-to-their-knees part of their routine—which is *not* the modified version agreed upon—and Porkchop lunges forward, dragging Elena behind him. His leash catches Preston behind his calf, and when Preston trips, Elena's end of the leash flies from her hand.

"Oh s***," Elena's father says as the room erupts in pandemonium.

Porkchop, as big as a man, but far shorter and rounder, charges through the crowd. Some kids dive out of his path, while others scream and clutch one another, even if they're nowhere near him.

"Porkchop, no!" Elena cries.

"Tranq him!" shouts Chance.

"Bite his ear!" Olivia shrieks.

"Omigosh, omigosh, omigosh," Yasaman repeats.

Katie-Rose takes off after Elena, Elena's dad, and Porkchop, and in her flurry of hero-fantasies, she sees herself jumping onto Porkchop's broad back and bringing him down. She *will* bite his ear, if that's what it takes.

"Out of the way," Chance says.

"Yeah, let a real man take care of this," Preston says, sticking his foot out to trip her.

Katie-Rose flies forward and lands hard on the carpet. Tears spring to her eyes.

Yasaman dashes over and kneels beside her. "Are you okay?"

"Everyone, sit down!" Elena's dad commands, so loudly and sternly that the kids who weren't sitting already do so now, with the exception of Chance and Preston, who keep chasing Porkchop like the wild boys they are.

"Don't make me get the ax, Porky!" yells Chance.

"You're scaring him!" Elena wails. "Daddy! Make them stop!"

Porkchop makes a rooting movement with his head and gallops in circles. Kids squeal. And Yasaman ... Where is Yasaman? She was there, right beside Katie-Rose, and now she's not. Where did she go?

"I'm calling animal control," Ms. Westerfeld says faintly.

Elena's dad squats and slaps his thighs. "Porkchop. Here, boy."

Porkchop pauses. The whole room holds its breath. Even Chance and Preston stumble to a halt, and just like that, Mr. Emerson is behind them, his expression foreboding. With his one hand, he grabs both boys by their collars.

"Ow," Preston says.

"I think you two are done here," Mr. Emerson says grimly. He glances over their heads at Elena's dad, who slaps his thighs a second time.

"Come on, boy," he says to Porkchop. "You're okay."

The room is quieter now. Porkchop lets out a funny sound, like a cross between a sigh and a snort, and trots to his master. Elena's dad picks up the end of the leash and wraps it around his hand. Everyone cheers.

"Kids," Elena's dad says, holding out his free hand like a police officer. "A little quieter, 'kay?"

"Yaaaaaay," everyone whispers.

Mr. Emerson guides Chance and Preston toward the wall and tells them to sit right there and not move a muscle until he returns. He walks Elena and her dad out of the building, and everything must be okay, because Katie-Rose can hear Elena's dad laugh at whatever Mr. Emerson says to him.

"Everyone, out to the playground," Ms. Westerfeld says.

Kids scramble up and head for the doors that lead outside, chatting in loud, excited voices.

Katie-Rose gets to her feet, too. She shares a wide-eyed look with Milla and Violet, because is that it? Just *"out to the playground,"* and the whole Snack Attack is over?

"Where's Yasaman?" she says.

"No clue," Violet replies. She laughs shakily. "Omigosh. Can y'all believe that just happened?"

"Why did Olivia say to bite his ear?" Milla asks.

Yasaman appears from the hall where Ms. Perez's room is. She's breathless, and she's got two spray bottles in her hands. Katie-Rose squints. They're . . . *perfume bottles*. What is Yasaman doing with perfume bottles at a time like this?

She's glad when Violet says, "What's with the perfume?"

Yasaman doesn't get the chance to answer. Ms. Westerfeld strides over to the four of them, and Yasaman hides the bottles behind her back.

"You four, in my office, now," Ms. Westerfeld barks.

The girls jump at her tone, and Ms. Westerfeld closes her eyes. She keeps them closed for quite a while. The flower friends glance at one another.

When at last Ms. Westerfeld opens her eyes, she says, "Actually, I've changed my mind. I need some alone time. So, girls, I want the four of you to sit back down and think about what you've done while I go to my office." She pins each one of them with her gaze. "I'll call you when I'm ready for you."

She goes to her office. She closes the door. The girls sit back down on the floor and try to be appropriately solemn. They succeed for five whole seconds before breaking into nervous giggles.

"We are so expelled," Katie-Rose says.

"Don't even say that!" Milla says.

"She's not going to expel us," Violet says. "She's going to give us a lecture, a *long* one. And we might, like, have to clean toilets or something."

Yasaman wrinkles her nose. "She'd make us clean toilets?"

Violet indicates Chance and Preston, who are sitting against the opposite wall playing paper football. "Betcha they get in worse trouble than we do."

"Unlikely," Katie-Rose says bitterly. She's sick of the way they've been treating her, sick of her own inability to turn it around and give them a taste of their own medicine. "They never get what they deserve."

Yasaman's eyes widen, like she's just remembered something. She gets to her feet and pulls up Katie-Rose. She hands her one of the perfume spritzers and says, "Come on."

Katie-Rose gets a sweaty feeling. "What? Why?"

Yasaman drags her over to the boys. She aims the Enchanted Orchid bottle at Preston and sprays.

"*Aaaaah!*" Preston yells. He recoils. "What *is* that?"

"Dude, you stink!" Chance says.

Yasaman lifts her eyebrows at Katie-Rose. Katie-Rose's pulse is racing, but she spritzes Chance anyway. She spritzes him and spritzes him, squeezing the lever repeatedly.

"What the . . . ? I smell all girly!" he cries, trying to wipe the smell off.

"Yasaman, stop!" Preston cries, and Yasaman sprays him again.

"Will you stop being mean to Katie-Rose?" Yasaman demands.

"Yeah, will you?" Katie-Rose says. Exhilarated, she

pushes the nozzle of her spray bottle, and another cloud of Blushing Cherry Blossom envelops Chance. "And stop pretending you're scared of me?"

He coughs and violently waves his hands in front of his face. "But I *am* scared of you!" He turns to Yasaman, his expression communicating utter shock. "And *you,* Yasaman. Who *are* you?"

She glances at Katie-Rose. "Katie-Rose's best friend," she declares.

"Yeah!" Katie-Rose says. She's so happy, she squirts Chance again.

"Truce!" Chance says. "I beg of you!"

Katie-Rose looks at Yasaman. "What do you think, bestie?"

Yasaman grins. "Oh, why not?"

Together, they address the boys: "Truce."

Thirty-seven

Camilla

Ms. Westerfeld doesn't expel them. She doesn't even suspend them *or* make them clean toilets. She does tell them they're going to have to stay inside during recess for the entire next week and, as Violet suspected, she gives them a long talk about school safety and appropriateness and the difference between standing up for something you believe in and staging a protest for the fun of it.

"But . . . we do believe in it," Milla says. Violet and Yasaman look at her in surprise. Katie-Rose, however, gives her a small smile. She squeezes Milla's knee without letting Ms. Westerfeld see, and this gives Milla the courage to continue. "We're sorry things got out of hand—"

"So sorry," Yasaman interjects.

"So so so sorry," Katie-Rose says.

"But Happy Healthy Farms hurts animals," Milla finishes. "And that's bad."

"The food they make hurts humans, too," Yasaman says tentatively.

"Because of the trans fats," Violet says. She glances at Yasaman, then back at Ms. Westerfeld. "Did you know that the Cheezy D'lites we have every day for snack don't have a single bit of cheese in them? Not one bit?"

Ms. Westerfeld wrinkles her brow. "Well, that's rather disgusting."

Milla nods. "It *is*. You should really stop buying them."

Ms. Westerfeld sighs. "It's more complicated than that," she says, and off she goes on a grown-up *blah blah blah* speech about budgets and feasibility and the challenge of finding healthy snacks for 250 students a day. The bottom line is that she's not getting rid of the Cheezy D'lites.

Yasaman slumps, and Milla can sense that Katie-Rose and Violet are sinking as well. When grown-ups get like this, it's easy for a ten-year-old to feel she has no power. Milla knows that's not true, though. She's seen her friends in action. She knows how powerful all three of them are.

Ms. Westerfeld eventually winds down. "So you understand, then, girls?"

Yasaman looks down. Violet folds her arms over her chest and stares away. Katie-Rose opens her mouth, then decides, apparently, that she's gotten into enough trouble for today and closes it without saying anything.

"Good," Ms. Westerfeld says. She takes in their disillusionment and frowns. "It's not a situation I'm thrilled about, either, girls. I hope you know that."

Milla inches her hand up.

"Milla?" Ms. Westerfeld says. "Do you have something else to add?"

"I know everything can't always be perfect, and sometimes we can't change things." *Like Stewy,* she thinks.

"That's right," Ms. Westerfeld says. She sneaks a peek at her watch.

"But sometimes, maybe, we just think we can't change something, and so we don't even try?"

"Hmm," Ms. Westerfeld says, and it frustrates Milla, because what that *hmm* means is, *And you are just a child, and children don't know the ways of the world.* Except that's just not true. Multiple thoughts go through Milla's mind in a quick progression: Jelly-Yums, Cyril being poked, Natalia's shiny buttons. Yasaman's sister, Nigar. Violet's mom.

Kids know way more about the world than grown-ups think they do.

"My mom knows a woman whose husband works at an organic food store," she says. "It's called Yummy Tummy."

Ms. Westerfeld raises her eyebrows.

"They make cheese nips, too," Milla goes on. "Only they're called Quacker Smackers. They're shaped like ducks."

"Aw. Cute," Yasaman says.

"Do they have trans fats in them?" Katie-Rose asks.

Milla shakes her head.

"Do they have *cheese* in them?" Violet asks.

"They do. Last night I looked them up online, because

345

I was sick of everything being bad. And, well, Quacker Smackers are good."

"Hmm," Ms. Westerfeld says, but it's a very different *hmm* this time around. This time it's her purposeful principal *hmm.* "Can you get me the name of your mom's friend, Milla?"

Milla nods eagerly.

Ms. Westerfeld presses her hands on her desk and stands up. "All right. I'm not promising anything, but I'll look into it. And now it's time for you girls to go back to class, don't you think?"

She escorts them to the door and watches to make sure they really do head to class.

"Yay!" Yasaman whispers as they walk. She lightly claps her hands. "Milla, you're amazing!"

She smiles.

"You really are," Katie-Rose says. She glances over her shoulder. "We'll talk more at recess—Ms. Westerfeld's still watching us."

Katie-Rose and Yasaman veer off to Ms. Perez's room, and Milla and Violet continue to their own class. When they get there, Milla reaches for the doorknob.

Violet stops her. "Hold on," she says.

"Huh?"

"Just, there's something you need to do, and it's sort of like what I needed to do. With my mom."

"Huh?"

A wrinkle forms between Violet's eyebrows. "I don't know if I can explain it. But, like, this is your life, you know? And you can't shut yourself off, or hate yourself, or hate anyone else. Not that you do! That's not what I'm saying."

"Then what are you saying?" Milla says, the tiny hairs on her arms standing up.

"I don't know," Violet says. "Um, just trust me, okay? And stay right there."

Violet slips into the room and pulls the door shut behind her, leaving Milla by herself. Her spine tingles, because she might know—maybe—what Violet is hinting around about. And suddenly she's terrified, because she can't—she *cannot*—possibly do what Violet wants her to, even if she herself wants to.

She's got to get inside the classroom before Violet sets in motion whatever it is she has in mind. She opens the door to go in, but as she does, someone else comes out, and they collide.

"*Ow,*" Milla says, because the person steps right on her foot. And, of course, she's wearing delicate beaded ballet slippers, because she hasn't dared wear more sturdy shoes since the day she went to Max's, and her toe hurts so much that it takes her a couple of seconds to realize the person in front of her, who stepped on her foot, is Max himself, looking upset.

"Sorry," he says.

"No, *I'm* sorry," she babbles, hopping on her uninjured foot and cradling her possibly broken one. "Except, omigosh . . . *ow!*"

Max gives her a small laugh. "Owwie ow ow."

"Definitely." She stops hopping and lowers her owwie foot, doing her best not to put weight on her hurt toe. She looks at Max, and it's the first time she's truly done so since the day at his house. She drinks him in. First, his "I Read Banned Books" shirt, then his unruly brownish-blond hair, and finally his sweet, adorable, Colgate-y smile.

"Max," she says.

"Milla," he says.

There's an awkward silence. It goes on for a long time—too long—and at the same time, they blurt, "I just wanted to say—"

"You first," Milla says.

"No, you," says Max.

"No, really, *you*," Milla insists.

"Oh good Lord in heaven," Violet interjects, making Milla jump. She's got the door to Mr. Emerson's room open just a crack, and she's sticking her head into the hall and eyeballing both of them.

"I told Mr. Emerson you have some private business to dicuss, but you've only got five minutes."

Milla is mortified. "Violet!"

"What?" Violet pulls Milla close and says, right into her ear, "Just tell him you're sorry and hug him!"

Milla begins to hyperventilate. "I can't!" she whispers, panicked.

"Yes, you can," Violet says. She raises her voice. "Max, is it okay if Milla hugs you and tells you she's sorry about Stewy?"

Max's ears turn bright red. "Um. I already know she is."

"See?" Violet says. "Now good-bye." She gives Milla a hard look, as if to suggest that though her work is done, Milla's is not. She disappears into the room and shuts the door.

Max directs his attention to Milla, who can meet his eyes, but just barely. "Milla, I know you didn't mean to."

"You do?" Milla says.

"Of course. Who would step on someone's hamster on purpose?"

Feeling slightly better, Milla lets her shoulders unhunch from up by her ears. "A deranged Girl Scout?"

Max laughs.

Violet pops out again—*good grief, does she have her ear pressed against the door?*—and gives Milla a hefty shove. "And now, hug time."

Milla flies forward, and Max catches her. He feels solid. He *is* solid.

"You okay?" he asks, helping her right herself.

"Other than being totally humiliated?" she says, aware of how hot her face is.

"Other than that, yeah."

"Um, I guess."

"Good," he says. He smiles goofily.

She giggles. He is adorable, and his hair is poofy, and his breath smells like—oh, joy—Colgate. The Great Regular Flavor.

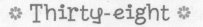

Thirty-eight

Lunch is made of awesome. Milla, Violet, and Yasaman are back together again, *and* there are two—count 'em, two!—snack-size bags of Doritos in Katie-Rose's lunchbox.

"Hey!" she exclaims, pulling them out and displaying them. "My mom must have given me Sam's Doritos by mistake." She hugs both bags to her chest. "Mine, mine, all mine! *Mwahaha!*"

"But Katie-Rose, they have trans fats," Yasaman says.

"They do? How do you know?"

"Because it says so on the label," Yasaman says,

turning one of the bags over to show her. "The only chips that don't are SunChips, Fritos, and Lay's Potato Chips. I learned that when I learned about Cheezy D'lites."

Milla, Katie-Rose, and Violet let this information settle over them.

"Wow," Violet says. "Somewhat impressive, somewhat scary."

"But I don't have SunChips or Fritos," Katie-Rose explains. "What I have is Doritos. And I love Doritos." She pauses. "Do the Doritos people support factory farms?"

"I don't know," Yasaman says. "Milla, do you?"

Milla shakes her head. "I can find out tonight, though."

"Terrific," Katie-Rose says. "In the meantime, since we don't know, and since they're already here in my lunch, I'll just go on and eat them."

She opens the first bag of Doritos and shakes some into her mouth. With her head tilted back, she happens to see the table behind her, where Natalia is sitting with Ava and Olivia. Only to say "sitting with" is an overstatement, as it's more like Ava and Olivia are their own duo, and Natalia is just . . . there. Nibbling on her sandwich. Sipping her . . .

OMIGOSH, COKE! She's sipping a Coke! Right there in front of God and the world and everyone! Katie-Rose grabs Yasaman's arm and shakes her so energetically that Yasaman's grape flies out of her fingers and hits Milla's forehead.

"Ow!" Milla says.

"Natalia. Is. Drinking. A Coke!!!!" Katie-Rose cries. She stands and does a butter-churning, booty-shaking dance right there in the lunchroom. "Liar, liar, pants on fire! Natalia is a big fat liar!"

"Katie-Rose, sit down," Yasaman says, jerking her back into her seat. *"Hush."*

"But—"

"No," Yasaman says. "You have to stop being mean to Natalia. In fact, you have to do more than that. Katie-Rose? You have to be *nice* to Natalia."

"But—"

"She doesn't have to be your best friend. She doesn't have to be *my* best friend." She pauses. "She's not a flower, after all."

Katie-Rose glomps on to that like a bee to honey. "That's right, she's not. So why do I have to be nice to her?"

Milla shakes her head.

Violet arches her eyebrows, letting Katie-Rose know she expects better of her.

"Because of exactly that," Yasaman says. "We're really lucky, Katie-Rose, because we have each other. She doesn't."

Katie-Rose growls, though deep down she knows Yasaman's right. And to *show* Yasaman she knows that . . .

"Hey, Natalia," she calls, projecting her voice.

Natalia lifts her head and stares at Katie-Rose in alarm.

"Come here," Katie-Rose says.

Natalia tries, unsuccessfully, to hide her Coke behind an apple.

"You can bring your Coke," Katie-Rose says, rolling her eyes. "I'm not going to say anything about it. I promise."

Natalia gathers what remains of her lunch. With her lunch bag in one hand and her Coke in the other, she approaches the flower-friends' table.

"You can sit with us if you want," Katie-Rose says.

Behind her enormous headgear, Natalia is wary. "Ith thith a trick?"

355

"*No*, Natalia," Katie-Rose says. "If you want to sit with us, sit. If you don't, don't."

Yasaman smiles at Natalia.

Milla pulls out a chair.

Violet says, "You have a little, um . . ." She subtly indicates her teeth.

Flustered, Natalia starts picking at the cracks. "Did I get it? Am I okay?"

"It's still there," Katie-Rose says. "What *is* it? Omigosh, it looks like a—" Her eyebrows go up to her hairline. "Natalia Totenburg, have you been eating Green Apple Sour Loops?!"

"No!" Natalia protests, but her wild eyes give her away.

"Na*ta*lia," Katie-Rose says. "There is green-ness in your braces. There is the distinctive smell of green apples on your breath. You have been drinking Coke and eating Green Apple Sour Loops. Admit it!"

"Is that your whole lunch?" Violet marvels.

"No, of courth not," Natalia says. "I had a pack of . . ."

"Yessss?" Katie-Rose says.

Natalia closes her mouth. Her tongue moves around

behind her upper lip, and it looks like she's rolling marbles around in there.

Katie-Rose makes a *go on* circle with her hand. "Coke, Sour Loops, and . . . ?"

"Cheeth and peanut butter crackerth," Natalia mumbles.

Katie-Rose slaps the table. "The bright orange ones that come six to a pack? Dude! I *love* those!"

"Gross," Yasaman says.

"They're not made by Happy Healthy Farms, are they?"

"No!" Natalia says indignantly.

"Excellent," Katie-Rose says in her president-of-the-world voice. "Then let's move on." She lifts the second bag of Doritos. "So, Yaz, can I eat these even though I've already had one bag?"

"Well, Katie-Rose," Yasaman says, "you need to ask yourself if you really think that's a good idea."

Katie-Rose closes her eyes, concentrating hard. She opens her eyes and grins.

"Okay," she announces, ripping open the bag. "I said yes."

"You're going to have Dorito breath, you know," Yasaman says.

Katie-Rose munch-crunches, and it's loud, because Doritos *are* loud. Then she leans into Yasaman's face and says, "Yesssssssss, my precious. I just thank my lucky stars you love me anyway."

Saturday, September 24

Thirty-nine

The Flower Box.

The*rose*Knows: 'ello, dahlinks! Do I sound British?

MarshMilla: do u WANT to sound ~~British~~?

The*rose*Knows: I dunno. do i?

ultraviolet: Mr. McGreevy is British. he's cool.

The*rose*Knows: ooo, that drinkie makes me thirsty. Thirsty and hungry!

The*rose*Knows: wld somebody make me some yummy treats, plz?

ultraviolet: u put in a whale icon, k-r. u can't eat a *whale*.

The*rose*Knows: meh. Whales don't have trans fats, do they?

MarshMilla: they might not have trans fats, but they have BLUBBER

The*rose*Knows: mmmm, blubber. Me lub blubber.

ultraviolet: and here is me about to throw up at that: 😧

ultraviolet: and, 2 seconds l8r, here is me officially throwing up: 💀

Yasaman: ewww!

MarshMilla: hey, yaz, good job on the whole Snack Attack campaign.

Yasaman: thx. *u* did more than I did, tho

The*rose*Knows: now, now, we ALL did a good job, girls.

ultraviolet: we did, didn't we? and not JUST with the Snack Attack, either.

The*rose*Knows: meaning . . . ?

ultraviolet: well, I was scared to visit MY MOM, but I did it anyway.

MarshMilla: and i made things right with max . . . even after . . . you know.

Yasaman:	**and Katie-Rose, u did something biggish 2. U stopped being mean to natalia.**
The*rose*Knows:	weeee, how exciting
Yasaman:	**I'm proud of all of us, which is why i made a special speekee just for us**
The*rose*Knows:	and no one else?
Yasaman:	**and no one else**
Yasaman:	**ready?**
ultraviolet:	ready
MarshMilla:	ready
The*rose*Knows:	ready!!!!
Yasaman:	**ok, i'm pasting it in. or i shld say pasting *her* in, cuz Siggy the Frog is a she.**
ultraviolet:	oh, siggy. how we love u, siggy.
The*rose*Knows:	yes, yes we do! Altho I actually kinda forgot all about that silly frong till this very moment. Shhhh! Don't tell!
ultraviolet:	ahem. siggy is not a *frong*.
MarshMilla:	I don't even know what a frong is
The*rose*Knows:	+hits self in head with cookie tray+
The*rose*Knows:	forgive me, SIGGY THE FROG. I luv u very much, SIGGY THE FROG!

ultraviolet:	I think it's 2 late, katie-rose. I think u scared siggy off . . .
Yasaman:	**ag! technical difficulties. 1 sec!**
MarshMilla:	speaking of love . . .
ultraviolet:	yessss?
The*rose*Knows:	smooch-smooch, max-max! 😜
ultraviolet:	pucker up, sweetie!
MarshMilla:	u guys! NO!
MarshMilla:	i mean, yes, but . . . grrrrr.
MarshMilla:	i'm talking about ms. perez and mr. emerson. wldn't they be so cute together?
The*rose*Knows:	hey, we shld get them toegether! That shld be our next project!
MarshMilla:	~~i think that's a GREAT idea. i'm totally in.~~
The*rose*Knows:	+pulls fist into side+ YES!
The*rose*Knows:	Vi? u in?
ultraviolet:	sure, it'll be fun 😎
The*rose*Knows:	+dances around room, then runs out of breath and sits back down+
ultraviolet:	what about u, yaz? u up for operation teacherly lurrrve?

Yasaman:	absolutely, and it goes very well with siggy's special message to you three, which i will present to u NOW!
Yasaman:	or rather . . . NOW!
ultraviolet:	+twiddles fingers+
MarshMilla:	violet, shush
ultraviolet:	what?
Yasaman:	it shld pop up in a sec, i swear.
Yasaman:	ah, here we go!

ultraviolet:	helloooo, siggster!
Yasaman:	u have to double-click on her, all at the same time. on three . . . two . . . one . . .

> Hello! I am Siggy, and I am a FROG. And do u know what FROG stands for? Forever Rely on Your Girlfriends!

MarshMilla:	awwwwww! yasaman!!!!!!
Yasaman:	wait, there's more

> LUV U,
> MY FLOWERS!

ultraviolet:	yaz, u rock. and i think i speak for all of us when i say what i'm about to say. right, girls?

MarshMilla: um, i think so, if what yr about to say is what i *think* yr about to say . . .

The*rose*Knows: ok, that was way too confusing. I will make it easier. YES!

ultraviolet: in that case, let's all say it together, even if I'M the one typing the words.

ultraviolet: LUV YA TOO, YAZ! 🖤 🖤 🖤

The*rose*Knows: and u!

MarshMilla: and *u*!

Yasaman: **+lip quivers, but in a good way+**

AND U !!!!!!!!!!!!!!!!!!!!!!

Acknowledgments

I am blessed with so many amazing people in my life, and I'm full to the brim with gratitude. Strike that. I'm not just full to the brim; I am overflowing with gratitude, and it's bubbly and sweet and never-ending, and yes, it makes me a bit sticky, but these things happen.

Special fizzy thanks to:

Girl Scout Troop 814, especially Sophie, Becca, Ashley, Brittany, Sheridan, BreeAnne, Anna, Rhiannon, and Sidney. Wh-hoo! Dead chicken dance! Porkchop the pig! Yeah!

All the kids, teachers, and staff at Rivendell: Um, can anyone say "total inspiration"?

My Starbucks peeps, who tolerate my random inquiries and keep me caffeinated to boot: Angie, Seth, Ian, James, Brittany, Michelle, Audrey, Christy, Bre, Carly, Jack, and yes, Terace and Ari, too (because y'all might as well be Starbucks peeps, pint-size or not!).

My medical expert, Jim "da man" Shuler, who answers my oddball questions without batting an eye, even when they involve the sad event of, erm, something really sad happening to one of God's wee creatures. (May he rest in peace.) (The wee creature, not

Jim. Because Jim is still alive, and may he stay so for ninety-six more years at least.)

My Girl Squad: Chelsea, Kayce, Brittany, Amy, Sara, Stephanie, Church Lauren, Sieglinde, and Julia (even though she's still in Thailand, the rat). Thanks for loving my kids, unloading my dishwasher, folding my laundry, and generally keeping my life on track. Y'all are made of awesome.

My lady friends: Jackie, Nina, Holly, Maggie F., Maggie A., Gini, Julianne, and Sarah. Oh, sweeties, you hold me up. (And praise the Lord, you also ply me with margaritas and peanut butter chocolaty treats! Wh-hoo!)

My lady friends who are also my writer friends, and who are also sexy-foxy-fab: stylish Sarah Mlynowski and the dignified Emily Lockhart Jenkins. You two are my darlings, and I would be . . . a pea without you. A tiny, sad, shriveled-up pea, crying green pea tears. Y'all make me a better writer and a better person. Best of all, you make me giggle. A LOT.

My water cooler buddy, Bob, who's always there to offer sanity and support, hugs and high fives.

My intrepid agent, Barry Goldblatt, who had no idea what he was getting into when he signed me on, but who has stuck with me through thick and thin, dramas and traumas, tampons and smooching and bras, oh my!

My Abrams peeps: dashing Chad, debonair Scott, elegant Tamar, cutie-pie Maggie, creative Maria, superfresh Brett, funky Maz, that handsome devil Jason, manly Michael, and—be still, my heart—my glorious, brilliant, wise, and warm editor, the one and only Susan "Pigtails" Van Metre, who looks so adorable in her newsboy cap. (Susan's parents? Y'all should be soooooo proud of your girl! I know you already are. But I'm just sayin'. Thanks for bringing her into this world!)

My fam: the whole crazy lot of ya! A bonus shout-out to Susan and Mary Ellen, for keeping our own goofy childhood alive. To Sarah Lee, for making me muffins. To both my dads, whom I will designate as Country Dad and City Dad (though neither of you is mouselike at all): Country Dad, you always nurtured my tomboy spunk and (occasional) fearlessness, which I passed along to Katie-Rose; City Dad, you are a model for unflinching self-examination and the willingness to take on new challenges, even in your dotage. Kidding! +insert City Dad guffaw-slash-wheeze-slash-red-faced-hacking-fit here+

And Mom, you are everything I aspire to be. Well, except for the tailored outfits, which you pull off beautifully, but which would look really stupid on me, and anyway, I'm happier in jeans. But jeez Louise, Mom, I love you so much. Thanks for loving me back.

Finally, Jack and Al and Jamie and Mirabelle. How could I exist without you? I couldn't. Y'all are the moon and the sun and the stars; ice cream and kettle corn and playing in the park; hugs and kisses and nose rubs. But Jamie and Al? Enough with the fart jokes. Really. And Jack, stop encouraging them. As for you, Miri-Potato, come sit on my lap and let me brush your hair, because even though you resemble a street urchin, you will always be my little girl. ♥ ♥ ♥ ♥ ♥